# Western
# Sadhus and Sannyasins
# in India

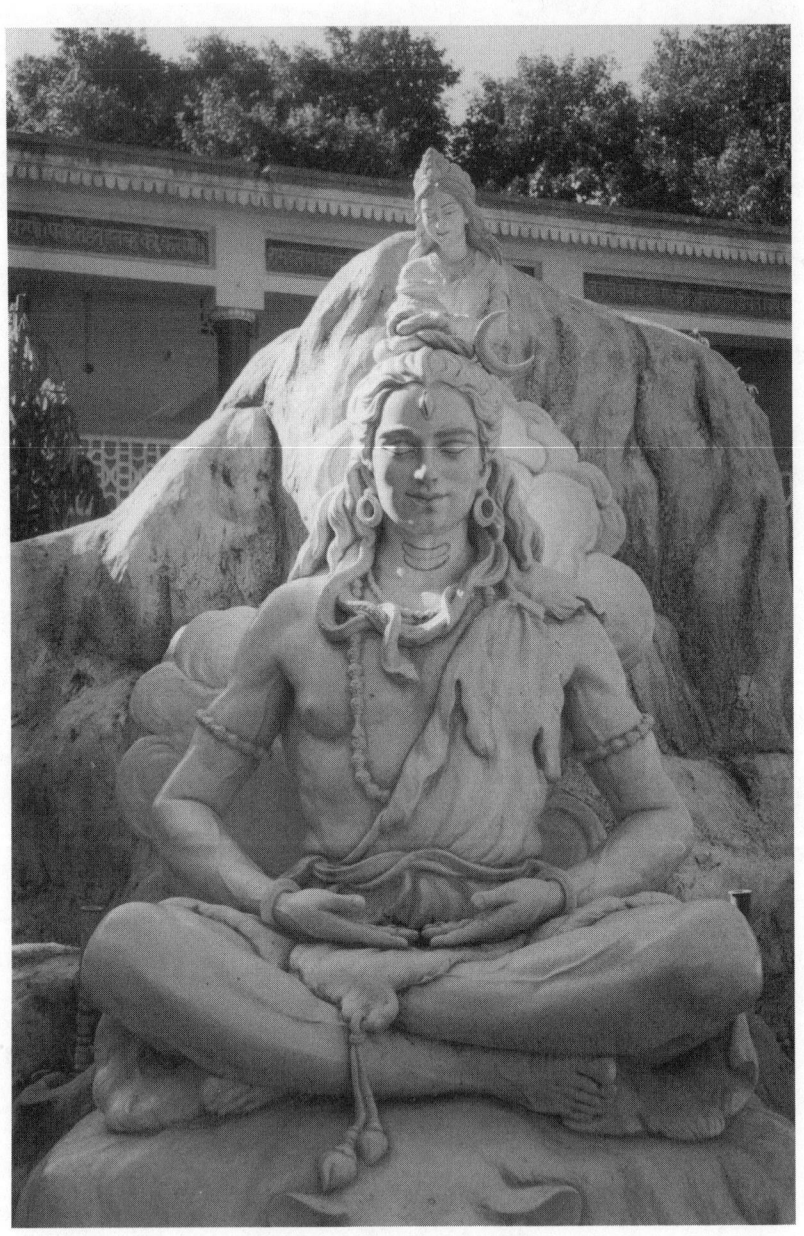

Lord Siva, the ultimate *sadhu*

# Western
# Sadhus and Sannyasins
# in India

Marcus Allsop

HOHM PRESS

Prescott, Arizona

Cover design: Kim Johansen
Cover photo: Marcus Allsop. Hanuman at Virbadra temple, Rishikesh. Lord
    Siva is believed to have incarnated as Hanuman to serve Lord Rama
    during his earthly sojourn. Hence his presence in many Siva temples.
Layout and design: Shukyo Lin Rainey

Library of Congress Card number: 00-101868


ISBN: 0-934252-50-5

HOHM PRESS
P.O. Box 2501
Prescott, AZ 86302
800-381-2700
http://www.hohmpress.com


This book is printed in the U.S.A. on recycled acid-free paper using soy ink.

This book is dedicated to Yogi Ramsuratkumar,

the God Child of Tiruvannamalai,

to Mr. Lee Lozowick,

to an anonymous *aghori sadhu*,

and to Mother India.

## Acknowledgements

I would like to give thanks to the many individuals who provided hospitality, help and kindness during my stay in India preparing this book. They include: Jacques Vigne, Penny Leishman, Kundali Dasa, Kesava Priya, Govindaji, the Swamis of Akhand Lxya Dham, Kamala Das, Bhim Singh, Brett, Michael of Vrindivan, Jay Bihari Sharan, Saksi Gopal, Mrs. L. E. Singh, Swami Jnaneshvara Bharati, Neem Karoli Baba Ashram in Vrindivan, Anandamayi Ma Ashram in Kankhal. I thank my editor, Regina Sara Ryan, for her hard work and encouragement.

Finally, a special thank-you to Liz Attawell for generous help in the production of the this book's original manuscript. It would have been a tough job without you, Liz.

# Contents

# Preface

India is a country that once visited is impossible to forget. She has a special magic that seeps into even the most casual visitor. I have felt keenly the attraction and pull of India in my own life since I first visited in 1989, eager to experience something other than the familiar. Grandiose and naïve it may sound, but I was looking for the meaning of life. What I encountered was a series of intense shocks and shattering circumstances that showed me clearly and absolutely the futility of the methods I was using to search out that meaning.

Chastened, I returned to London and attempted to find an answer to the conundrums and experiences India had provided me. I longed to go back, though at the same time, was scared to. India was, after all, utterly overwhelming.

Nine years later I returned, yet probably a day had not passed in that time that I did not think of or yearn for India. Circumstances for a return were not right until November 1997, when I traveled there to join my spiritual master who, with a party of his students and friends, had journeyed to India to visit his own guru. In my spiritual master and his guru I had found a lifeline to the meaning that previously eluded me.

The idea for this book arose during this memorable trip. Specifically, I saw a Western *sadhu* deep in meditation at the gates of Ramana Maharshi's ashram in Tiruvannamalai, a small city in southern India. I was moved by the sight of this Western man—who had obviously renounced his former home—immersed in the Indian tradition.

At the time I did not disturb him, nor later could I find him. But the next day, during *darshan* * with my guru's master, the idea of interviewing such individuals for a book flashed into my mind.

Days later, when my guru and his party returned to their respective countries, I set about the task of searching out India's Western *sadhus* and *sannyasins*. Beginning in Tirumvannamalai, this search took me from the deep south of the continent to the Himalayas in the far north, with stops at some of the holiest pilgrimage sites in India. While I thought there would be many such people, I found only a few. Nevertheless, some of the many facets of India's rich spiritual culture opened up for me in this journey. My hope is that all who read this book will share in that experience. The testimonies of the *sadhus* and *sannyasins* I met bear witness to the extraordinary opportunity for growth that India offers to those who approach her with sensitive appreciation.

(*) Most italicized words are explained in the Glossary, pp. 197-201.

## The Questions

In the interviews contained here I put the same questions to each of the *sadhus* and *sannyasins*:

- "How did you come to be in India?"
- "What attracted you?"
- "Who was your guru?"
- "What was their teaching?"
- "What kind of *sadhana* do you practice?"
- "Do you fulfil a teaching role?"
- "What is your attitude toward the West?"

Often, these questions served only as an occasional prompt, as the interviewees covered many issues before they could be asked about them. I found that some of the interviewees, having renounced their former lives, were, understandably, unhappy to talk about them. Therefore, I had to use discretion on each occasion to "feel around" what was acceptable to each person.

Similarly, details of an individual's personal practice, or his or her relationship with a guru, were not always forthcoming. Where there are few details in those areas, it is at the interviewee's request.

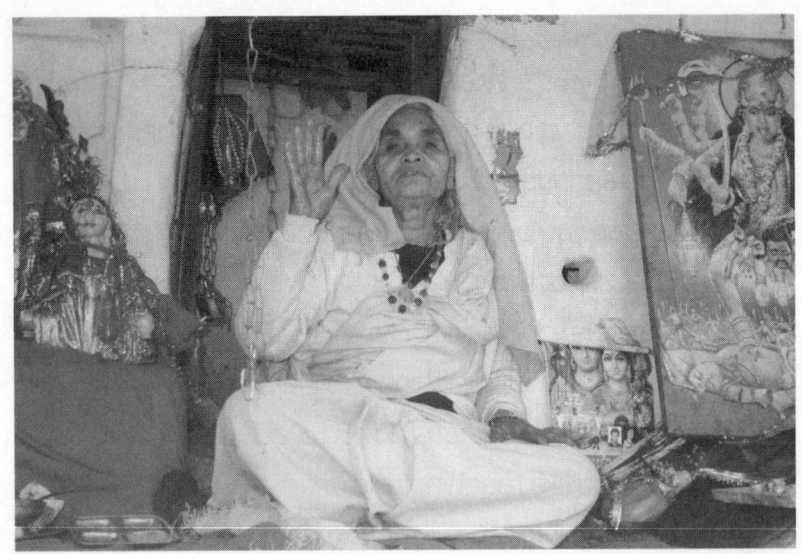

Blessings from an Indian *sadhini* seated outside her *kutir* on a hilltop in Haridwar.

# Introduction

Far, very far back in the mists of time, millennia before recorded history, India was home to legions of wandering mystic ascetics. Across her sun-graced land, they chose a radical alternative to the conventional approach to life dictated by the societies of their day. Century after century, up until this present day, they have plunged deeply into an experiential quest for the true meaning of human existence. In thick green jungles, icy mountain caves, and throughout India's arid plains, *sadhus* and *sannyasins* have pursued transcendental union with the cosmic principle that originally created them; they have sought for the living knowledge of, and merging with, God.

The first mention we have of these pioneers of the soul is found in the sacred revelatory texts of the *Vedas*, the world's most ancient spiritual scriptures, traceable to 1500 B.C.E. However, to historically localize these texts is to do them an injustice, for the *Vedas* were never intended to be written down. Rather, they were to be recited, heard, and meditated upon.

# INTRODUCTION

The *Vedas* and their *mantras* are believed to be direct sound emanations from the Cosmic Source. These sound emanations are ever present and were simply discovered by sages, or *rishis*, during their meditations. The *rishis* passed on their discoveries on for the greater good of the world. Accordingly, the *Vedas* have no human author. Their proper intonation is an exacting science, and their chanting is the primary duty of the Brahmin caste. That a special sect of people existed for the recitation of the *Vedas*, and to some extent still exists, should come as no surprise when one grasps the ultimate significance attributed to the *Vedas* by the Indian people. The sonic vibrations of the *Vedic mantras* teach humans of their ultimate nature, reveal the presence of deities, and produce a powerfully harmonizing effect in the atmosphere. Basically, their constant chanting is believed to be of such immeasurable value that without it the world descends into spiritual darkness.

The descriptions of ascetics within the *Vedas* are not different from descriptions of many *sadhus* and *sannyasins* one may encounter in India today: long matted hair, ash-covered, clad in simple rags or hide, bodies and foreheads anointed with purifying symbols, few possessions—including a staff and *kamandal* (water pot). The *Vedic* ascetics were in all likelihood associated with *Saivism*—worship of Siva; Vaishnava *sadhus*, those who honor Vishnu, developed later. Although bearers of antiquity, *sadhus* and *sannysins* are not considered old-fashioned or outdated, for the realization they aspire to is timeless. Today, India is home to an estimated four to five million *sadhus* and *sannyasins*—a tiny fraction of whom are Westerners.

The term *Hinduism* is a label given by foreigners to India's wide practices of religion. A more correct term is *sanatana dharma*—the eternal path—but actually the Indian scriptures do not refer to the faith by any name. This religion is unique by virtue of the fact that it has no single historical founder, unlike Christianity, Islam, Buddhism, Jainism or Sihkism. Rather, this eternal path is an accepted primeval way of living in harmony with cosmic forces. A galaxy of spiritually illuminated men and women have left various imprints on its interpretation and practice.

Saivites and Vaishnavites have their own scriptures, temples, festivals, holy places, rituals, and ascetic sects. Although some sectarians insist on the maintenance of a distinct line of separation between the two, even suggesting they are actually different faiths, this is far from the truth. Sacred texts of both sects evolved after the *Vedas,* and their authors make many reverential references to them, with no attempt to disdain or disqualify the *Vedas* in any way. Both have their *dharmic* roots deep in the *Vedas,* which clearly state that the one truth reveals itself in the form of many deities. Sri Ramakrishna (1836-1886), one of modern India's most highly revered sages, attested to this particular revelation. Ramakrishna explored the *sadhanas* of the various world religions, abandoning himself to the intense and exclusive practice of each one for an indefinite period. He included both Christianity and Islam in his explora-

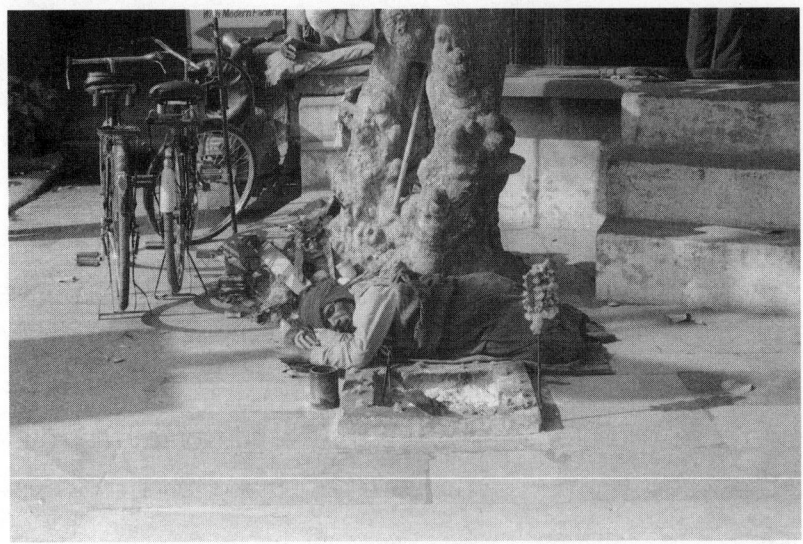

By the ashes of his *dhuni* (sacred ritual fire), an Indian *sadhu* takes an afternoon nap.

tion. When he took initiation into one path, he completely dropped the beliefs of the others. Time and time again he was blessed with the rarest, spectacular visions and visitations from God in the forms of Siva, Krishna, Jesus, or whichever divinity he was engaged in worshipping. Time and time again these fantastic and beautiful presences would dissolve into that one primordial light, which is pure and absolute love.

The first three interviews that follow all took place in Tiruvannamalai, a major center of spiritual activity for many centuries. Saints, *sannyasins, sadhus,* and seekers—both Eastern and Western—are drawn by the magnetic pull of Mount Arunachala, which is said to be a direct and full manifestation of Siva. Arunachala is surrounded by an extraordinary mystique, and the townspeople feel great devotion for their holy mountain. Hundreds circumambulate it daily; during my visit I witnessed a *sadhu* who was lying on the dirt road with his arms horizontally joined over his head, rolling his way around the mountain as an act of *tapas*. His body was soft and fluid, joyfully surrendered to his task, allowing him to proceed over the rough ground without resistance and bruising. From loud speakers and folks' lips the *mantra: Arunachala Siva, Arunachala Siva, Arunachala Siva, Arunachala* is heard everywhere.

Mythology has it that Siva appeared in Tiruvannamalai as a blazing column of pure white light to appease a quarrel between Brahma and Vishnu. Unable to decide who was the greatest deity, a mighty fight broke out (on the kind of cosmic scale one might expect from the creators and preservers of this universe!). Siva was notified by worried *devas*, so he manifested as a miraculous flame and declared that the greater divinity would be the one who could first discover either the flame's base or summit. Vishnu assumed the form of a wild boar and burrowed deep into the earth, while Brahma became a swan and flew far into the sky. Neither met with any success, and returned after arduous journeys, humbled by the infinite majesty of Siva's light. This column then diminished in size, and for the sake of the world to have its holy vision, took the form of a smaller flame. This smaller flame was known as the *jyothir lingham* and appeared in the *satya yuga*. During the *treta yuga* it became an emerald hill; in the *dwapara yuga* it was a golden

hill; and in this *yuga,* the *kali yuga,* the hill of granite we see
today.

Built at the foot of the mountain and dedicated to the worship of Siva is the massive Arunachaleswarar temple. Its ori-
gins can be traced back to the ninth century, the time of the
Chola dynasty, and it has been a site of continuous prayer and
ritual since then.

Sri Adi Shankaracharya, the renowned sage who reformed
the *Vedic* tradition, spoke of Arunachala as Mount Meru—the
center of the universe. In more recent times Sri Seshadri Swami
(1870-1929) resided here, and was widely regarded as a great
*siddha* of some eccentricity. Sri Seshadri Swami would jump
into passing rubbish carts, declaring them his coach, and enter local stores only to disturb the goods and rifle through the
cash box. A rise in sales was usually guaranteed after such a
visit! Seshadri fits the classic picture of the Divine Madman who,
though a miracle worker, chooses to live in rags, God-intoxi-
cated and homeless.

Better known as a sage of Tiruvannamalai is Sri Ramana
Maharshi who arrived in the holy city in 1896, and remained
until his *maha samadhi* in 1950. He wrote much devotional
poetry praising the transcendental nature of Arunachala—
whose name had been reverberating within him since childhood.
Sri Ramana Maharshi was a proponent of the path of *jnana,*
utilizing self-enquiry based on investigation into the question
"Who am I?" Shortly after his arrival in the city, the young

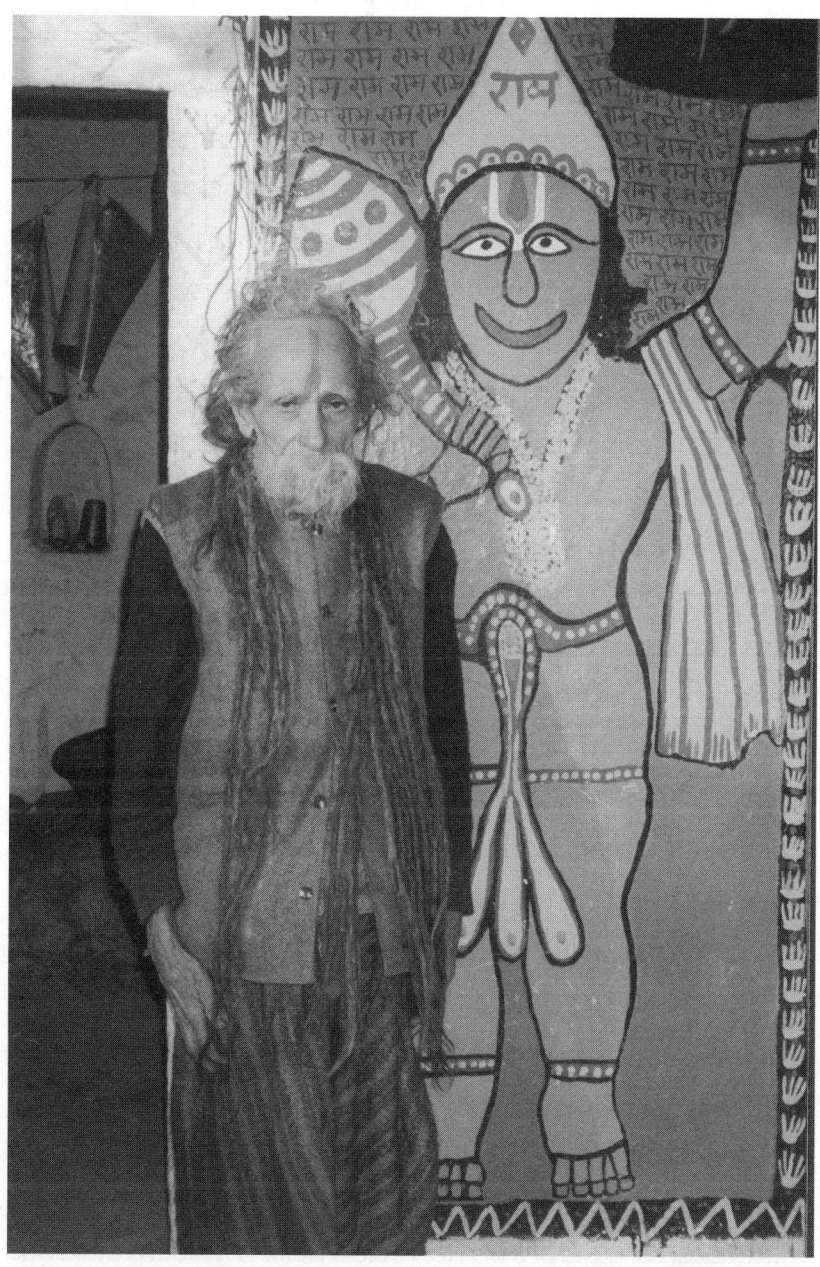

A one-hundred-year-old Vaishavite sadhu, whom the author came to know only as "little maharaj," outside his kutir in Vrindivan. Behind him is a folk painting of Hanuman, the monkey-god and servant of Ram.

## INTRODUCTION

Ramana took refuge in a dark and dank underground basement of the Arunachaleswarar temple's thousand-pillared hall. Here he could meditate undisturbed by the rough games of the local street boys. Entering into a deep state of mystical absorption, he was oblivious to the bites he received from the ants and vermin that proliferated in that cold vault. After two months, Sri Seshadri Swami discovered Ramana's plight and extended his protection toward him. The *samadhi* shrines and ashrams of both of these Masters are places of strong spiritual influence and upliftment.

Today, a third great sage is acknowledged in Tiruvannamalai. Yogi Ramsuratkumar lives here as he has for several decades. His inexplicable behavior of collecting rubbish and calling himself a filthy beggar had him labeled for long years as a deranged simpleton. Penny Ma, one of the *sadhus* I interviewed, recalled that to enter Arunachaleswarar temple one would sometimes have to step over Yogi Ramsuratkumar, if indeed one had not already stepped on him, as he had the habit of lying prostrate in the dirt. Now he is widely recognized as a great soul with an extraordinary capacity for transforming the lives of his thousands of devotees, and is affectionately known as the "God Child" for his innocent ways and joyous infectious laughter. Yogi Ramsuratkumar's recognition was assisted by the last Shankaracharya of Kanchipuram—one of the most revered and outspoken protectors of the *Vedic* tradition modern India has seen.

Close to the ashram of Ramana Maharshi, an enormous

temple—empowered by Yogi Ramsuratkumar as a place of worship and spiritual transmission for generations to come—is near to completion.. When it is completed, the Divine beggar has stated he will leave his body.

At the time of my visit to Tiruvannamalai the festival of Deepam was being celebrated with full pomp and ceremony. Deepam commemorates that auspicious moment when Siva appeared as the *jyothir lingham*. The holiday's climax is marked by the lighting of a huge oil lamp on the peak of Arunachala mountain. The town, which is busy at the most ordinary of times, becomes a sea of humanity during the festival, as devotees pour in from all over India for ten full days of worship. The streets are tightly packed, and the mood is both chaotic and ecstatic—the crowds eager to receive *darshan* of the temple deities Annamalaiyar, Unnamulaiyamman, Vinayagar, Murugan and Chandikeswarar. These radiant golden deities are slowly hauled through the streets surrounding Arunachaleswarar temple on huge gold and silver chariots festooned with colorful fresh flower garlands, thick and long as boa constrictors. The frequent explosion of firecrackers adds to the frenzied cacophony blaring from the scores of loudspeakers, all competing to demonstrate their devotion with decibels. *Arunachala Siva, Arunachala Siva, Arunachala Siva, Arunachala*, the sound of the mantra gets under one's skin, and even into one's blood.

Of the *sadhus* and *sannyasins* interviewed in this book, Swami Satyananda, Swami Devananda, Swami Atmaswaru-

pananda, and Swami Jnanananda all belong to the ascetic order founded by Adi Shankaracharya, known as the *dasnaamis*
or "ten names." Shankaracharya took birth toward the end of
the eighth century, beginning his ascetic career at the age of
eight; his rise to prominence was meteoric. A brilliant philosopher, he traveled the length and breadth of India, engaging in
dazzling debate, breathing life back into the *sanatana dharma*
of Hinduism at a time when Buddhism and Jainism were becoming ever more popular. The Shankaracharaya was an ad-
vocate of pure *monism* or *Advaita Vedanta*, the philosophical
position that demonstrates that only Brahma is ultimately real—
all else being illusory by nature of its impermanence.
Shankaracharya saw the need for the various bands of Saivite
ascetics to become as organized as their Buddhist and Jain
contemporaries. He set about the work of reformation, form-
ing monastic headquarters at the four cardinal points of the
Indian subcontinent: at Joshimath in the north, Dwarka in the
west, Puri in the east, and Sringeri in the south. Additionally,
and somewhat later, a fifth monastic center was set up in
Kanchipuram, where it is generally accepted that he died at
the age of thirty-two, having accomplished his life's mission.
(Although originating from predominantly Saivite sects, the tu-
telary deities at both the Sringeri and Puri centers are forms of
Vishnu—Adivaraha at the former, and Jaganatha at the
latter.)

# 1

Away from the swarming activity of the Deepam festival's fervent, magical party I met Swami Satyananda Saraswati. I had noticed him going about his rounds on two previous occasions, and had been impressed by the stark simplicity he wordlessly communicated—a communication I felt in my body. This feeling stayed with me throughout our meeting, and indeed was strengthened by the power of his gaze, which transmitted sincerity, depth, and spaciousness.

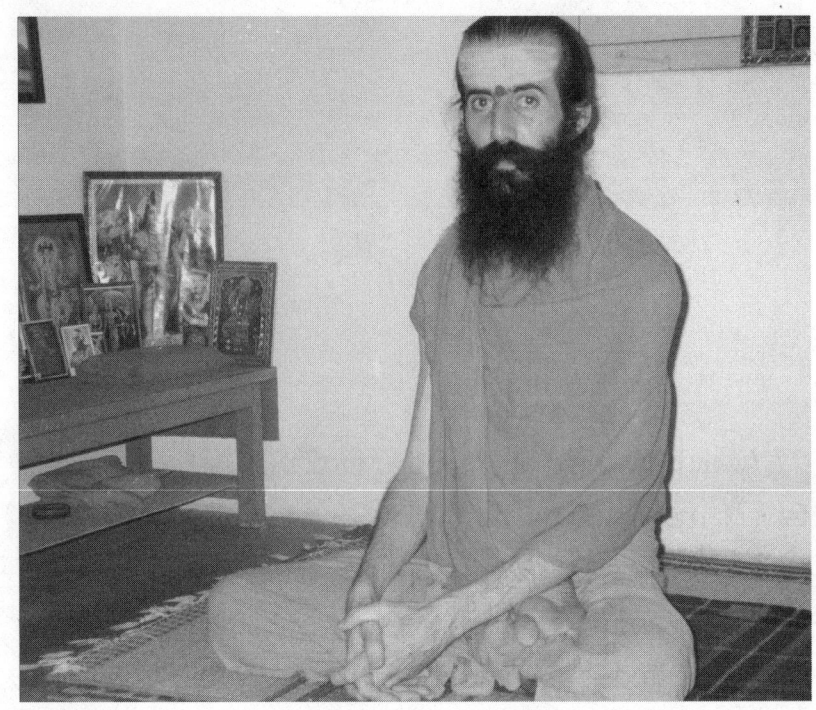

Swami Satyananda Saraswati

## Swami Satyananda Saraswati

As a teenager in Spain I was not interested in education, and had no ambition to start working without understanding what life was about. I am from a Roman Catholic background and reacted against that, trying to understand life through the senses—by which I mean different psychedelic drugs to expand consciousness. Quickly I saw that this was not the answer. Already at fourteen I had read the *Bhagavad Gita* and was practicing meditation, so this went on. Then later, at twenty, meditation deepened and I felt the need for some guidance. At that point I came to India, travelling overland; it took two months.

I came via the Punjab, and of course went straight to the Himalayas in search of a guru. Nothing happened. I met plenty of yogis, but not the expected guru, so I decided to travel south. In Bombay I met a seeker who was coming from the ashram of Swami Muktananda. This person did not like the ashram at all! However, somehow I was attracted and went to Ganeshpuri to see for myself.

3

My search was over. Although Muktananda was not there, a whole process started within me. Feeling no need to move, I just remained, and from here onward my path started.

I had arrived in India in 1976 and stayed with Muktananda until his *samadhi* in 1982. During this time I made a few return trips to Europe and spent a year with him touring America. I had expressed the wish to become a renunciate and a *sannyasin*, so, in 1980 he called me and said that if I was serious, it was possible.

I took the first initiation, *diksa*, that year and completed it in 1982.

Having taken the vows of a *sannyasin* you become a kind of dead man, as much as you can be. You perform the funeral rites during initiation. One ceases to work for money, and does not create a family; in fact one's only duty is to keep contemplating on the *mahavakya* you have been given. The *mahavakya* is a contemplative phrase (each *Veda* has one), and the phrase corresponds to the essence of that *Veda*. An example would be "Thou art That." All of the *mahavakyas* mean that you are Brahman, the Absolute, and this should be our awareness. You dedicate your life to your *sadhana* and get as little entangled as possible with the whole drama of the world. Of course some *sannyasins* create a big drama with, say, a mission, but they must feel that call from within, so it is their duty to do that.

Your guru is something you discover within through a person outside. Through Swami Muktananda I discovered the guru principle within myself. There is no way to thank him enough for this tremendous favor. Formerly I had been to teachers who gave various teachings and philosophies, but that awareness of Truth within me had not taken place. Muktananda always taught us that he was not the body, so I never understood the guru to be a person, even though the guru principle operates *through* a person. If one is sincere in practice, then guidance comes automatically; it all has to do with your eagerness and sincere desire for truth.

Nowadays my practice has changed. For many years I was sleeping less than six hours, waking at three A.M. for many hours of meditation, Sanskrit chanting, and thousands of *mantra* repetitions. When I came to live in Tiruvannamalai, for several years I circumambulated the holy mountain Arunachala every other day. Now, many of these practices have naturally fallen away. They no longer seem needed, though I maintain the greatest respect for them. I feel that many seekers want to grasp the highest Advaitic truth simply by the intellect, without ever having undergone serious *sadhana*, and that in most cases these people are deluding themselves. I see this here in Tiruvannamalai very often.

The condition I see more and more is that of the Western spiritual collector of gurus and initiations—going from master to master, ashram to ashram, without ever committing themselves to any path, *sadhana* or guru. They simply move around getting a hit from the *darshan* of each master, and they are going nowhere.

On the other side, I also see Westerners who come with the concept that there is no time, no path, no *sadhana*, as we are all the Self. Yet, of course, they need an air-conditioned room or they cannot survive! There is a lot of delusion and misunderstanding. I don't mean to say that these Westerners are not good seekers also, but I see a great lack of respect for Indian culture, manners, customs, and people. There is an air of stinking superiority.

The seeker should come to this land with a very humble attitude.

When Swami Muktananda was in his body I was teaching for him, coordinating all his activities in Europe. Creating ashrams in Barcelona and Paris, I traveled all over Europe giving intensives. But it reached the point where I felt that all of this organized, publicized teaching was a bit meaningless to me. I did it as a service to my guru. After his *samadhi*, however, I left his foundation, and have remained much more alone, quietly doing my practice. If I am invited to teach or give a talk in Europe it is only on an informal basis. There is nothing about the culture of the West that I miss and I have no particular attitude toward the future.

Years ago my only obsession about the future was that I

wanted to stay in India, but now I don't mind. I will accept my destiny wherever it takes me. I won't be throwing my passport into the Ganga! Once we have become one with the East within ourselves, even if we move to the West, the East is within us, and the East is the place of light and the rising sun.

For many of the seekers here, who isolate themselves or build castles around themselves in ashrams for many years, it is a very healthy exercise for them to try to withdraw in L.A. or New York. Then see if who they are is the same one, or is the external world changing their identity right away? I have found it helpful every time I have gone back to the West, because as long as our identity depends on externals we are weak and vulnerable. The goal of *sadhana* is to become strong and free.

I think that the difference between Eastern and Western spiritual thought is that no thinking person can reconcile themselves with the idea that if a man died on a cross two thousand years ago we must believe in him or be sent to hell for eternity. This idea that God has a chosen people, or only one prophet, one book, and that He manifests His truth to only a few chosen ones that the rest of us have to obey—these ideas are repulsive to any man with a minimal humanistic sense. Prior to Christianity, all the traditions—Eastern and Western—have a much broader view of God, of man and of the path by which man can realize God.

In particular, India has that very ancient tradition, unbroken

7

for thousands and thousands of years, with so many *rishis*, *mahatmas*, and great saints. There is definitely this quality in the land here, and within Hinduism. The real Hindu mind is a very open mind, a universal mind; it is in fact called *manushya dharma*, the path of mankind. It is eternal—an eternal *dharma*— and has never been closed, even though in some circles, mainly because of eight hundred years of Islamic invasion, foreigners are looked on with a little suspicion. For the most part I feel that my brothers have made me very welcome and have helped and supported me in case of difficulties of any kind. I have moved around a lot, been with the most orthodox Shankaracharyas, all kinds of *sadhus* and sects, and have felt as one with them. One of the things that breaks barriers is speaking the language. Once you know the language you begin to act and live the path as they do; you are one of them.

However, there is a great decadence occurring in the Hindu way of life due to the materialistic influences in the country. The goal of the people has become that of the West: to become wealthy and rich. Not rich in *dharma*, as in the olden days, which meant to live a very simple life. The powerful kings used to bow down to the naked renunciates, and the man of wisdom was the most highly respected.

Nowadays everyone bows down to dirty politicians and the whole of society here is under this influence.

At the same time that this is going on, temples that were

once poorly visited now have tremendous crowds. There is a certain revival happening. I pray it will have the strength to overcome all the obstacles to its fulfillment. But if I have to be frank, I'm not very optimistic about the future of Hinduism in India.

If Western people want to pursue a serious spiritual practice, I would advise them to start with a discipline they find a liking for and not to lose time going here and there looking for a guru. If you are serious in your practice then the guru will come. He need not be found in Varanasi, he can be found in New York. The true guru is, as I said before, a cosmic principle. When we really have need for it, it is there. That need requires sincerity in aspiration and eagerness in finding the truth, which implies the destruction of many things we cling to. If we are serious in this process, the guru will manifest and deeper guidance will come. Still, I would insist that the seeker stick to a path, tradition, and guru very much.

When you find your guru don't let him go! Even if you are with the wrong teacher, it is better to be faithful to that one teacher and pursue your *sadhana* with full focus than to roam around meeting one hundred good teachers without being committed to any of them.

# 2

What impressed me in meeting Swami Devananda for the first time was his deep seriousness and obvious learning. This rare seriousness was complimented by a wonderful and ready sense of humor, which I hope the reader is able to discern in some of his more peppery comments.

The home of Swami Devananda, like that of Swami Satyananda, was unmistakably that of a renunciate. The environment was clean and bare of all possessions, save for a few cane floor mats and a *puja* table—reassuringly austere. A sense of economy and contemplation could be felt. If I had been looking for any concessions to former Western lifestyles, there were none.

The authenticity of the two *sannyasins* I had met thus far, and their degree of integrity in embodying the ideals of *sannyas*, was really quite remarkable. Swami Devananda and I took *chai* together, pouring the piping hot liquid from metal beaker to bowl and back again to cool it. And there were biscuits—but not for Swami Devananda, only for the guest.

## Swami Devananda Saraswati

Taking *sannyasa* is a very strong *samskara* for me personally. I have always had this orientation. I remember at five or six years of age seeing a photo of a Buddhist monk in *National Geographic Magazine*. It was like a revelation to me, and I felt that this was a member of my true family. That revelation got lost in life—I was brought up in western Canada. I have always studied Christianity, but the study of its evangelical operations put me off!

In my teens I went over to Buddhism, mainly because the books were available, and for many years I was a kind of Buddhist. I would try to follow its ideals, as I understood them. Being a natural vegetarian I was always in conflict with the food habits in Canada. I left the family house when I was fifteen and never had much contact with them after that; there were no close ties. At nineteen I left Canada to travel the world and ended up in India, via Israel, in 1967.

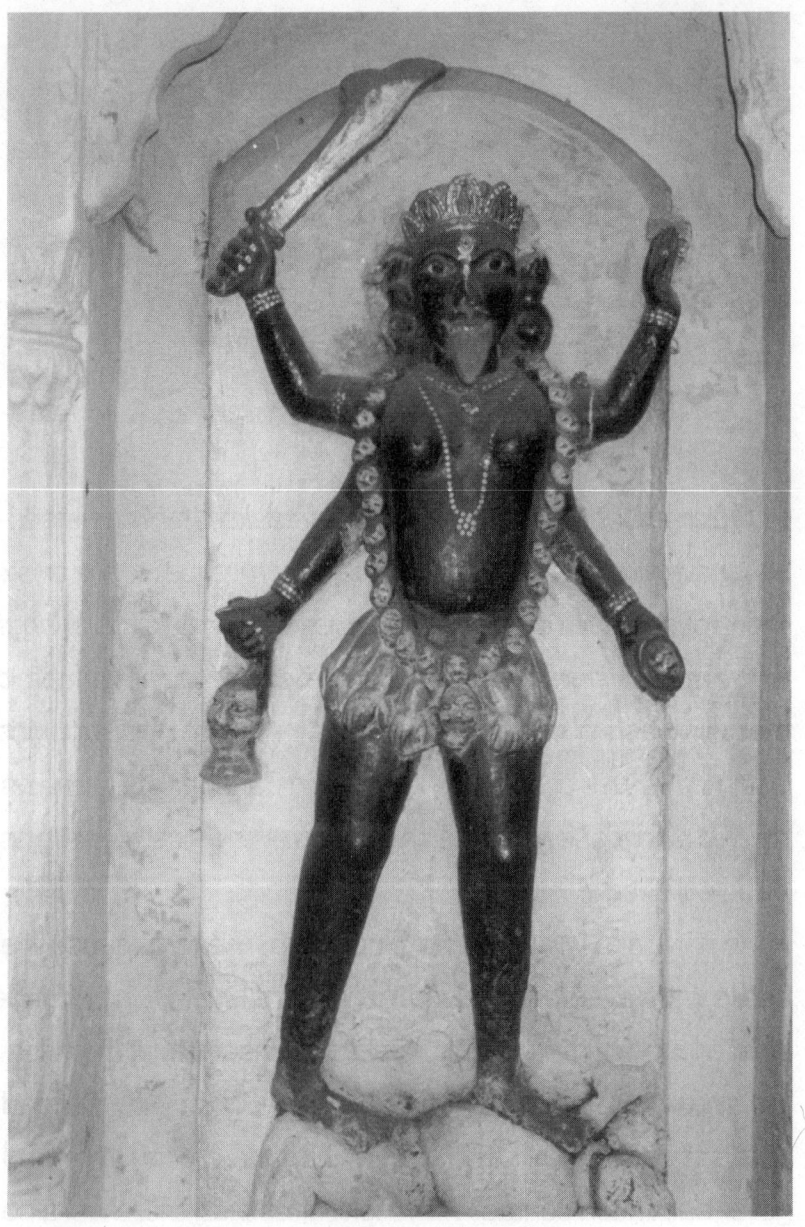

Kali, the Mother Goddess of Kashi.

I went directly to Kashi (Varanasi) and it was just like I had come home. I never wanted to leave the place again. It is very difficult to live in India, but so much is compensated by the psychic ambiance of the place. Since that time I have lived with *sadhus* and Brahmins only. Their way of life is completely logical and rational to me. It also means, of course, that modern Western civilization has no value to me at all. There is nothing I want in it. Unfortunately, it is the civilization that now dominates here in India. When I came here there were many motivating factors to push people out of the West, like the Vietnam war, which was not a direct factor but definitely had an influence. It created an opening by which many people could move around.

I am a devotee of the Mother Goddess and always have been. In Kashi there was a human level where She was available, rather than as a mental concept. Of course, the form of the Goddess in Kashi is Kali, which is very fierce. I have always been interested in history, it reflects the truth in a kind of distorted way. To me, there has to be religion that is natural to the cosmos, natural to the cosmic order. This somehow became available to me, and it is personified as the Mother Goddess. India is the last of the great pagan civilizations—a Hindu is an Indian pagan.

Varanasi was a kind of rebirth for me. Naturally I became very ill and had to leave the country, but I came back in one year. I could not stay out of India. Once more I ended up in

Varanasi looking for a teacher, and again almost died from some disease or another.

Reading *The Gospel of Sri Ramakrishna*, it was unbelievable to me that such beings were available in this age and that it was possible to contact these individuals. The necessity of having a guru began to plague me very much. Eventually I was guided to a mahatma in central India, whom I served for some years. Although he was a *tantric* teacher, he introduced me to a life of *Vedic* living, or *sannyasa*, and I became very sure that that was where I wanted to go. My original guru was not a *sannyas*, although he was a very great *yogi*. I wanted to take traditional *sannyasa*, but this can only be taken from another *sannyasi*, so one of my guru's disciples sponsored me.

I have great faith in this tradition. If it is understood sincerely it supports and *is* a guru in itself. Of course it gets perverted, and some discrimination has to be used to sort it out, but the basic tradition is always there to guide. What are you going to do when the guru goes? That is what the tradition is for, to guide and support.

My spiritual lineage comes from the first student of Shankaracharya; its authority is the *Upanishads,* which are short and readable. Shankara codified or attempted to reform the *Sannyasa* Order, due to the diversity present at that time. We believe he was influenced by the Buddhist orders, with which there is a great similarity. We are also called Smarta, which is the name of a Brahmin community. Shankaracharya set up four monastic centers which are called Smarta Mutts to distinguish them from the Vaishnava *sannyasis*. The Vaishnavas have the same kind of initiation we have, which is called Vedic. Its base is the Vedic authority.

*Sannyasa* also has a legal recognition; it is considered a rebirth and you are no longer entitled to inherit from your former family. Accumulated wealth or property must start from the point of this *sannyasa*, this birth. Age is also counted from this time of *diksa*. The hierarchy amongst *sadhus* has to do with the number of *chatarmas* they have observed. This refers to the four-month period during the rainy season, like the Buddhists observe, when *sannyasins* cannot move around, and are supposed to sit in one place. Generally they go back to the guru's house. Jain monks also follow these same rules.

Actually nobody takes *sannyasa* from anybody. You must renounce yourself; no one else can renounce for you. However, the guru's authority is needed to say you are suitable for renunciation. What happens is that there are so many frauds and imposters that the *sannyasin* has to name an authority for a time. He must be identified with a guru or *mutt* for authenticity.

*Sannyasins* also have a system of identification that includes ten or fifteen items with which, if one interviews another, he can identify the other's authority. Of course, this system has now been published and is available to anyone, but unfortunately that is modern life. So what can you do?

*Sannyas* is a *sangha*—a community. Our habits are similar. It worked very well in older times, and employed a very important social role in providing information carriers and teachers—not just an important role in religion. Unfortunately, the Islamic invaders destroyed it, as did the Marxist Rationalists in later times, and the British, who classified us as beggars. (For some reason Marxists in India always go after the British colonial mode of administration.)

I have lived thirty years in India, and am a kind of Indian, but in Tamil Nadu, where I live, there is a very rationalistic tendency, and the Brahman and *sadhu* community have come under great attack. For a long time the *sadhus, sannyasins, vairagis*—the seekers who have taken a direction in life—had nowhere to go, no place to be fed. *Sadhus* have to live in a sympathetic community that does not persecute them. That persecution has tailed off now, and some *sadhus* are coming back to Tamil Nadu, though much more remain in north India.

Even in Buddhist times the *sadhus*, petty criminals, and beggars all got mixed up together. In *Puranic* times, thieves took on *khadi* cloths, and nowadays Christian missionaries take on the *sannyasi* cloth to fool the locals. They cannot sell their soap powder straight across the counter!

The *sannyasi* is considered the embodiment of Hindu *dharma* and has to interact with the community in a certain way. When you get those who don't do this—who are either Christian missionaries or criminals—it harms the community. Missionaries have exploited Hindu hospitality. They have a very specific agenda—saving our souls! Yet, we don't want our souls to be saved by them, so this problem arises. Even as far back as the sixteenth century an Italian lord, Roberto De Nobili, came to India and forged palm-leaf scriptures to make a Christian *Veda.* To convert Indians to Roman Catholicism he posed as a Brahmin and even took a bath, a practice which was unknown to the Europeans at that time.

In one sentence, *I try to live in the presence of God.* How I do that involves different things. We say a *sannyasi* has one duty and that is to eat his food; he has no other duty. What this means is that he is supposed to maintain his life, and as long as his life is maintained every possibility is there.

All *sadhus* have their particular personal devotions, *japa,* meditation—their religious habit. This varies greatly among *sannyasins.* Unlike, say, a Christian monastery, we allow for a great flexibility in discipline, so development is accommodated. In Western monastic institutions one has to surrender to the doctrine, or leave. We are entirely the opposite. We will allow for every flexibility except three things (which also extend through the Jain tradition): one must not drink alcohol, eat meat, or engage in sexual activity. There is no way of bending these rules without the *sannyasi* getting into great difficulty, at least within

19

his own community. If he insists on a sexual relationship he has to leave *sannyas*. Tradition establishes a standard against which we measure everything. *Sannyasins* do not live in an ordinary time frame, they live in eternity. Although having all eternity, once we are on the path we will reach the end of it. As to the time on the path, that is for the Divine Mother to decide. We are only waiting for the grace of God.

Everything in the Hindu religion is a process of mental, psychic and physical purification—we do not separate the body from the mind. For example, when we wash our bodies we have faith that our minds are also washed—it is like that. We are bound by certain rules, like not revealing our inner life, but we have no external life! We do not seek personal or emotional fulfillment, which is what society wants. We seek a relationship with our Lord.

There is this great problem of personality in human life. All gurus have charisma, which they use, but this cannot be taken as an absolute. It is nonsense to rely on the outer. Our view is that there is a teacher for everybody on every level, however we always speak of the guru in absolutes. Within the *dharma* the guru has three functions. He is supposed to initiate—induct you into spiritual life with a look, *mantra,* or speech (but you must be a fit recipient). He is supposed to give *upadesh*, the instruction you are meant to follow. Thirdly, he is supposed to protect you on the psychic level. If he is a really great soul he does this because you are human and so is he. The guru will protect his own all the time. This is a very specific function. He is to be called on when you come across obstructions. Nowadays, the guru is treated as an idol in the negative sense.

Though our philosophies are unitary on a spiritual level, we think that there are differentiations on a human level. A dog, a cow, and someone's wife are not the same after all! There *is* a distinction of function, although they are one on an *atmic* level. This is where humanism falls down, however. Egalitarianism is a false concept entirely; everything is *not* the same. All religions may lead to God, but God has many aspects, and what aspect does a particular religion lead to? The *asuras* also worship God. Consciousness is on a scale of higher and lower forms. Was the consciousness of Mohammed the same as that of Vasya? You *cannot* say that it is all the same. Modern political social philosophies condemn us as elitist, but we are not. We understand the position of things.

I don't have a very good impression of Westerners who come to India. I feel the quality gets more inferior all the time. They are all God's children, but they bring the cult of individualism and personality that has turned them into nonentities. There is a great paradox in life whereby people who deny personality become much stronger in character when they deny themselves, as we understand it, psychologically. This strengthening doesn't always happen, of course, but mainly it does, because you allow the Divine to shine through. Before people judge us they should try to understand our tradition; and this is what most people lack. They come with solutions to problems they don't understand. Maybe I'm a little pessimistic; I'm sure some good must come from their contact with India. I understand that there is a culture shock. Unfortunately, that produces sewer inspectors who only see the dirt in the streets and hate India. Many of them are suffering from mental and emotional problems.

Here in Tiruvannamalai there is no human guru, as such. The *ishwara,* presiding deity, here is the holy mountain, Arunachala. It is very active on a psychic level, but if your psyche is not pure enough that can create a lot of problems. You find a lot of Westerners here who cannot relate even ordinarily, and there is no one around to pick such people up. Occasionally these people cut their wrists, throw shit at the walls, and are taken away by their condition. The great misfortune is that many Western visitors cannot put anything into context and have no understanding of Hinduism. They form their own fantastic opinions, and cannot understand what they are seeing, as they are responding to everything on the level of feeling, and are mad after experience. Experience comes and goes, so what do you do when it's not there? They are after *shakti* all the time and have ideas about magical mystical India, with snake charmers and rope climbers. They are baffled by the corruption of modern India. Of course India is only following the West in that field.

I know these people suffer terribly, psychologically, and they are looking for some relief from that. There is nothing wrong with that. Many people here find great solace in the writings of Ramana Maharshi, and that is a very great thing.

I find the ordinary travelers, low budget travelers, to be of much superior quality to the so-called seekers I meet in south India. They have a certain awareness about what they see and what they are doing. They also know what they want. I will also confess that I dislike the fact that they make no effort to integrate themselves socially, from the way they dress to the way they eat.

We know that we are in a traditional culture that appreciates a certain dress, yet Westerners insist on flaunting this. The Indian will go to any extent to be helpful and hospitable if you show even a little respect for their social or religious culture. To have a European come with some appreciation, they are completely forgiving, but that's not what most Westerners are doing here. They are on their own gratification tour of some kind. Whenever they have any doubts, we advise them to leave before they catch AIDS or cholera.

Most people living in a particular culture carry its mind contents, and this is brought *with* people. I'm not saying they should not come, but it is more their personal attitudes we would like to see changed.

There are a lot of strange Western characters in India, but they are getting reduced now because there are communities and teachers in the West. (They can lead a spiritual life in the West, if they have the means and the will to do so.) Also, many of them do not like modern India and its bureaucracy. When I came here thirty years ago there were a lot of such people. Many, many *sadhus* are just hippies, which, from a civilizational point of view, is great because they have been given a place to drop out and still be fed. The *sadhu's* life in general is very much a refuge. Even among *sannyasins* we believe this *khadi* cloth protects us and is a refuge. At the same time we have a responsibility toward it.

I will never return to the West. The ambience of the place does not suit me. Canada is like a great void to me, and there is nothing there I want. By the grace of God I have no teaching function, and I don't want one either. When a *sannyasi* walks down the road, his cloth is meant to be a teaching—it is a passive teaching function. The point is we cannot be ignored completely, which is the success of it.

India's role is that of a world Teacher. We are very interested in the *dharma* going to the West. (Never mind that India is failing in her teaching duty today . . . there is always tomorrow!) Now, the spiritual seeker (never mind the *sadhu*) does not have the support of society. It is quite true that in urban

India and the West people no longer feel they need religion. They no longer respond to the symbols of it, or to those who represent it, because they get their psychological and emotional support from secular services. Yet, this fails. In the West religion has failed because it has become secularized.

The seeker needs support or an environment to practice in. An ashram is a pure, benign place for a spiritual seeker to proceed. If this is not available, we must be strong enough to create our own circumstances. Hopefully, after years of *sadhana* a person can create that circumstance wherever they go. The great *mahatmas* can do that; they can go wherever they like and eat whatever they like without being affected. They can impose their circumstance in any situation.

However, there are geographical places that are natural manifestations of the Divine in the land itself. The pagans tend to have identified these places, and most churches and cathedrals are built on them. The Christians put their own label on the spiritual content of a place, but that's not what we want. We want the essence of it. There must be hundreds of such areas that have not been identified as holy places in the public mind as yet. The point is that these places support *sadhana* and the seeker, because they contain all kinds of beings, light, and deities whose whole job is to support and help the seeker. This is the nature of such holy places. You contact the Spirit through matter, like the Ganges, which we do not worship in itself but the Deity it is a manifestation of. Also, you get the benefit of the great *rishis* and saints who have done their *tapas* there. Even the acts of devotion of thousands of ordinary people add to the holiness of a place. In Sanskrit we have technical terms for all of this.

There are natural manifestations of the Divine such as holy hills. There are places where a great *yogi* has placed his *tapas* or energy into an image. There are the rituals and prayers of Brahmins who have brought the deity into a particular image. And then there is the *atmic,* which is what a person does with their own deity or image. In a holy place all of these energies are coming together. This is why we call all of this a science—it all has a rationale and a logic. This is the world *sadhus* live in. They respond to subtle things rather than to the human personality, and it is very difficult to understand their responses as a result of this. What we need in the West are people practicing right from the beginning. This has a tremendous effect on the whole consciousness. All of this has its import to make the world that we live in a better place. An airy-fairy universalism is not enough.

When you do *sadhana,* meditation, you need to have an armor, a *kavacha,* which you can always make ritualistically with your mind or by a prayer to your guru. You can do it with a mat, or a map of a physical spatial dimension. You can expand the *kavacha* from the mat, to the house, to the perimeters of an ashram. This armor then excludes negative energies, and the practice can then be done anywhere.

Meditation is dangerous, in a way, because one is opening up to all kinds of influences. So *sadhus* are always drawing boundaries around themselves. They do it with their own inhalation, drawing lines or sprinkling water—all of which is *tantra,* and it gets very elaborate. One extends one's place by the lighting of incense in front of one's deity. The material conveyor always acts as a conveyor for the spiritual side.

People who come here should not take, only. I understand that sitting smoking *ganja* and gossiping has a very important place in life [he smiles ironically], but creating psychic heat through *tapas* is tremendously vital, and *that* is contributing, giving to a place.

A great soul only *gives* to a place, whereas the seeker is still taking. But to become free we have to have no debt. Just to come to India and enjoy is not enough. Some work has to be done, a return made. The traditional Hindu is very aware of this debt creation, which is why *mahatmas* in ashrams require work from people also.

There is another side to spiritual places—all kinds of criminal elements gather there because they also belong to the Lord. Though one should feel spiritually secure where we are doing *sadhana,* the external struggle to survive will always be there.

## 3

    I met Satyananda Amritham in the *ashram* of Sri Yogi Ramsuratkumar where I requested her participation in this book. Although a time was not fixed, we met by chance a few days later in one of Tiruvannamalai's muddy back lanes, whereupon she invited me to her nearby home to conduct the interview. We passed through a shared courtyard into her tiny room, and I quickly commenced my questioning. Soon I became aware that I was in the company of someone who was something of a visionary. Satyananda Amritham appeared to me as having a strong sense of God as the Beloved, and in her company one felt that the form of the *Divine* might appear at any moment. Her eyes shone as she recollected the many ways her life had been touched. It was inspiring to see the fire of devotion alive in this *sadhu's* heart. As she described the extraordinary details of her journey one felt included, not only as a fellow traveler but also as a part of that same Beloved's play.

# Satyananda Amritham

I am originally from America. How I came to be living in India these past eighteen years is the result of a strong call. I had to come here. From the age of three up until seventeen I was loving God and doing everything in His service, seeing all beings as Him. I was taught very early. There was a lot of illness in childhood—a third of the time in bed with high fevers, lots of visions, and conscious dreaming. During this time there was a long inner association with people I later came to realize were Sathya Sai Baba and Mother Krishnabai. [Sathya Sai Baba is the world's most popular living guru, known for his well-documented miracles, dedicated charitable service and claims of being the *avatar*, or savior of the age. His followers, who run into millions, believe him to be an incarnation of Shirdi Sai Baba, the Maharashtran saint who died in 1918. Mother Krishnabai, who died in 1989, was the principal devotee and feminine counterpoint to Swami Papa Ramdas, the genial guru who advocated recitation of the name of God—*Ram Nam*—as the principle mean to God realization. Swami Ramdas died in 1963, and today their ashram in Kanhangad, Kerala, still resounds with twenty-four hour a day repetition of the *mantra: Om Sri Ram Jai Ram Jai Jai Ram.*] From the age of four I was with Mother Krishnabai, inwardly, many times. She told me that she was my godmother. She had a spinning wheel with golden thread, and she gave me a thread and said this connected my heart to hers. She sang the *mantra, Om Sri Ram Jai Ram Jai Jai Ram,* and gave instructions directly—how to do everything perfectly, doing everything for God, and seeing that God was manifested in all forms.

At the age of seven up until ten I was living near Mount Shasta, California and had many visions of Sathya Sai. I didn't know who he was—just this amazing teenage boy who gave teachings. We played together in the hills and he materialized things in conscious dreams of great power and luminosity. That land and this land are *all* dreams, they are all mind. This waking dream is simply a longer dream. When the mind is completely still, everything disappears—nothing is seen.

So, the life up to seventeen was very God-centered—loving all and feeling all beings were my family. But I really did not understand what happened to adults; why they seemed so unhappy and treated each other so harshly. I saw people working so hard for material things that did not even bring them satisfaction.

Around eighteen there was the sense that since I was in society, since the body was in this society, it was important to learn about it; to learn why people were the way they were. I also learnt not to speak about my inner experiences. I read Yogananda's *Autobiography of a Yogi*, and it was the first time I found reference to people who experienced the same things I did. I started to listen to Alan Watts on the radio. My teacher at the time, who had been to India, said I must read the *Bhagavad Gita* and the *Upanishads*. Amidst this, I was learning about the world, worldly life, and I got married and had a child. I took many different kinds of jobs, in an intense search to find a means of work where I could evolve and help other beings evolve too. The closest thing seemed to be teaching and mime. There was a period of intense illness, again, which led me to study naturopathy and healing. I practiced that for about five years.

In 1977 I went back to college to finish a degree in theatre arts and found myself in a class that was a research project about the effects of Rolfing and the Alexander Technique on human beings. I joined a Rolfing-Feldenkrais group. This was a profound and powerful integrative inner experience of the life and spirit. There were some very vivid experiences of moving consciousness from this time and place to another that was equally vivid in all the senses, as vivid as this. I felt as though this was what I had been looking for and started working on prerequisites—studying anatomy, physiology, and biochemistry very

33

intensely for two years. I wrote the required paper, was accepted for the first half of training, and then I practiced bodywork for one year in New York.

For three years there had been a number of processes—inner processes—that seemed like I was being prepared for death. All of the karmic relationships with people seemed to come to completion, each very peaceably, beautifully, and clearly. Looking at every event in the present and past life, there was a time when I was shown everything right back to the beginning, and was engaged in clearing it—forgiving, expressing gratefulness. I was moved by life and God into the here and now, and really into a Oneness with everyone I met, as if I were them and they were me. About six weeks before I came here I kept hearing this little voice saying, "Come to India." I said, "Why should I come? You come here all the time and I'm happy." (I was referring to the presence of Sathya Sai Baba.) I'd had a spiritual teacher named Owen James for a year and a half in New York, and I consulted him about it. He said I should go to India and stay for as long as I could. It was a clear call, I came in 1980. When the plane crossed over India there was a powerful feeling of coming home, a powerful experience of peace that I did not expect to find in the world. I knew it from inside only. People came up to me and said, "You're going to Sathya Sai Baba, come." I was taken to Whitfield and spent a year there, a time of immense peace and silence and love. For much of the adult life I had refused to sit in meditation because I wanted the same experience all the time, so in the last few years only I took a meditation practice. I just sat trying to comprehend the vastness of Sathya Sai Baba's consciousness. There was no need for contact with the form, no need for outer contact. A very powerful teaching was given though by look, thought, and touch. The feeling pervaded: "I am one cell in the heart of God. The whole world is His Body."

However, at one point a clear call came to come to Arunachala in Tiruvannamalai. The call went on for forty-eight hours. I responded and arrived at Ramana ashram. It was the full moon, and a *chakra puja* was going on. I was given a room, and the feeling was the same as that at Sathya Sai Baba's ashram. No different! It was the same peace and love. I felt the same toward Bhagwan Ramana Maharshi as I felt to Baba. I was on fire, and I thought, "How can this be? They are two different forms. This is not single-pointed devotion to the guru." I had been very, very careful about this; there had been a strong inner warning. However, when I closed my eyes I'd see the two forms melting into one flame.

Later I saw very clearly that this one flame is in the heart of everyone, and everyone is thus one flame. There I had the experience, very strongly, that there is no death. Ramana's presence was as strong as if he were in the body.

I stayed in Tiruvannamalai for some time before returning

to Sathya Sai Baba and becoming a *sannyasin* in Bangalore. The desire for *sannyas* had come up previously, and when I gave Baba letters about it he said, "Wait. When the fruit is ripe it falls from the tree of itself." I'd also heard him respond to someone who had asked if they should take *sannyas*. "When there is any question about it, you should not," So I waited and observed the desire.

There is a kind of *sannyas* known as *vidvat sannyas,* that comes at the prompting of God. It simply happens and you have to do it—the blessing is very powerful. This occurred. Some days later Sathya Sai came back to Whitfield, blessed some saffron cloth for me, and said, "Very happy, very happy." He gave a profound inner experience of *diksa.* Mother Krishnabai later said that I had had only two unfulfilled desires when I came to India. One was to be with an incarnation of God and the other was to live as a *sadhu:* to live with no concern for the body, just to see everything as God and to trust Him absolutely, always singing and talking about Him, and knowing all places as home.

At this point all possessions were given away. One white sari came, then another, and saffron dye. It happened to be *Guru Purnima* [a once-yearly celebration dedicated to the advent in the world of the enlightened master. It usually occurs during the full moon of July] and I was invited to celebrations with three hundred *sannyasins* at Swami Nityananda's ashram outside Bangalore. We were given food and fifty rupees each in an envelope. Six older *sannyasins* came over to me and blessed me. It was immensely joyful. There were only two Westerners there.

After a few months I came back to Arunachala and stayed several years, doing traditional practices: six months of not sleeping more than three nights in the same place and not staying in anyone's home. For a number of extended periods I was not handling money—I wasn't begging because the instruction from inside and out was to never ask for anything, but to trust that whatever was needed would be given.

It was some time before I finally met Mother Krishnabai, whom I still did not associate with the godmother who had come to me so often in visions as a child. I wanted to meet her because someone had asked her why she took care of so many people and she had replied that taking care of other bodies was no different from taking care of her own. Everyone was herself.

I was taken to Ananda Ashram at a time period when Mother Krishnabai had said that no one should come due to a very bad astrological conjunction. When I was finally taken to her room, I recognized it from previous visions I'd had in New York of a room with big windows, hospital-green curtains, furniture covers, and a soft chair with a picture of a fat man in it wearing white. This, of course, was Swami Papa Ramdas. Mataji told me that Sathya Sai Baba was my guru. I have to say it's all a big mystery to me.

After this I lived in Lucknow for some time, where distinctions of high and low, spiritual and worldly, these concepts, were eradicated. I came to feel that if there is an experience of Oneness with everything, why would I play a role that sets me apart?

I returned to Tiruvannamalai in January 1987. Here I became aware of how powerful and subtle a background influence Yogi Ramsuratkumar has been during my time here. I met him the first time I came to Tiruvannamalai. He is a great saint who has not left this place for years. Whenever there has been any kind of need he has appeared and something has been cleared up very quickly, openly, and amazingly. We would just meet in the street. But if I planned to meet him nothing would happen. Just with a silent prayer in his ashram his blessing would be given.

There is the inner feeling that it is important to go back to the West at some point in the future. Only that way will my life and inner experience be integrated totally. This feeling keeps arising, but it has not been powerful enough yet to move the body! I have a desire to be in a community. Really, all that is important in every moment is to be fully present with full love and integrity in Oneness.

# 4

From Madras, or Chennai as it is now known, I made the thirty-eight hour train ride to Varanasi, the legendary City of Light. The city, also known as Kashi and Benares, is a full-blown assault on the senses, like no other I encountered in India. There is a sharp aggressive edge in the teeming city, a feeling of electric intensity and high tension. Sparks fly readily, and flashing displays of temper are not uncommon. Here the pressure is turned full up, and all the elements usually associated with India—noise, dirt, color, commerce, beauty, deformity, decay, purity, and piety—are somehow . . . more! Varanasi is simply more Indian than anywhere else in India.

I had been warned of frauds, cheats, con men, and thieves of the highest skill and caliber, so it was with some trepidation that I entered the Kashi Mandala—the energetic environment that surrounds this powerful spiritual city. Certainly it was true that there was plenty of awkward sidestepping and hard talking to be done, and yet this city is kind and gracious to the pilgrim who will bear its many surface hassles. To paraphrase

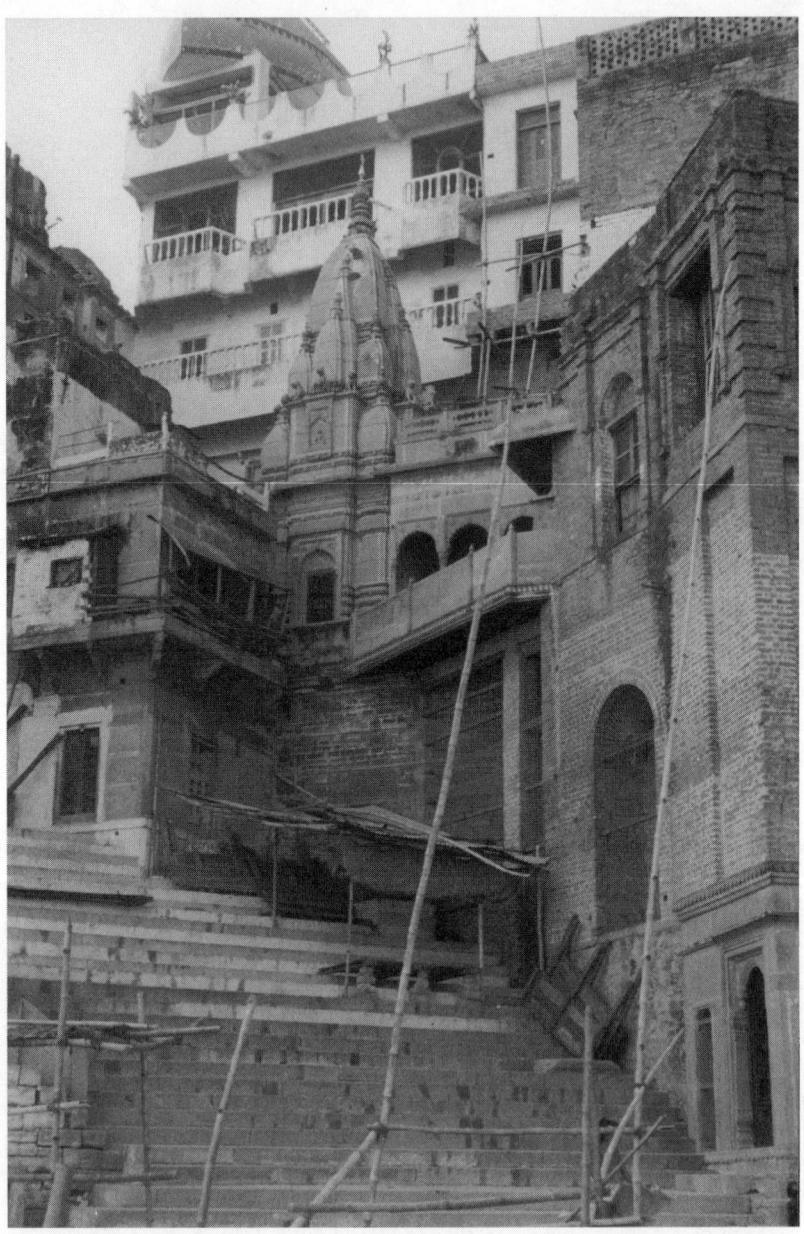

Chaotic and harmonic at the same time, the riverfront temples and homes of Kashi (Varanasi) seem to permanently teeter on the verge of collapse.

that paradoxical Western mystic, Gurdjieff, one could say of Varanasi that "all its sins are on the surface."

The dark warren of murky lanes that lead a rambling route to the bathing *ghats* are so narrow that only people and cows can pass. Losing oneself in this intimate and seemingly medieval maze is inevitable. Besides, in this decrepit and vital universe one soon becomes grateful for the loss. Each corner turned presents new vistas of exotic stimuli to feed all of the senses. Half-dressed children play, their eyes black with smudgy kohl; poor flower-sellers string a few saffron marigold garlands together; fragrant steam vaporizes around busy *chai* stalls; artisans sculpt and solder; ornate doorways open into crumbling temples where bells ring and incense burns.

Sooner or later the Ganga River is glimpsed through some ancient passage, drawing you down to the *ghats*. Here one can understand exactly why Varanasi is considered to be so holy, so pure. The sweeping river is a heart-stopping, beautiful sight: wide, majestic, and peaceful. Everything stops when you approach her shores, her mystic silence both seductive and ravishing. The presence of Siva, Lord of Ascetics, pervades the riverbank, and indeed saturates the entire city. This is the abode He vowed never to leave, and this is the place where thousands have been blessed with His vision. Varanasi was once known as The Forest of Bliss; sadly the trees are long gone—but the bliss remains.

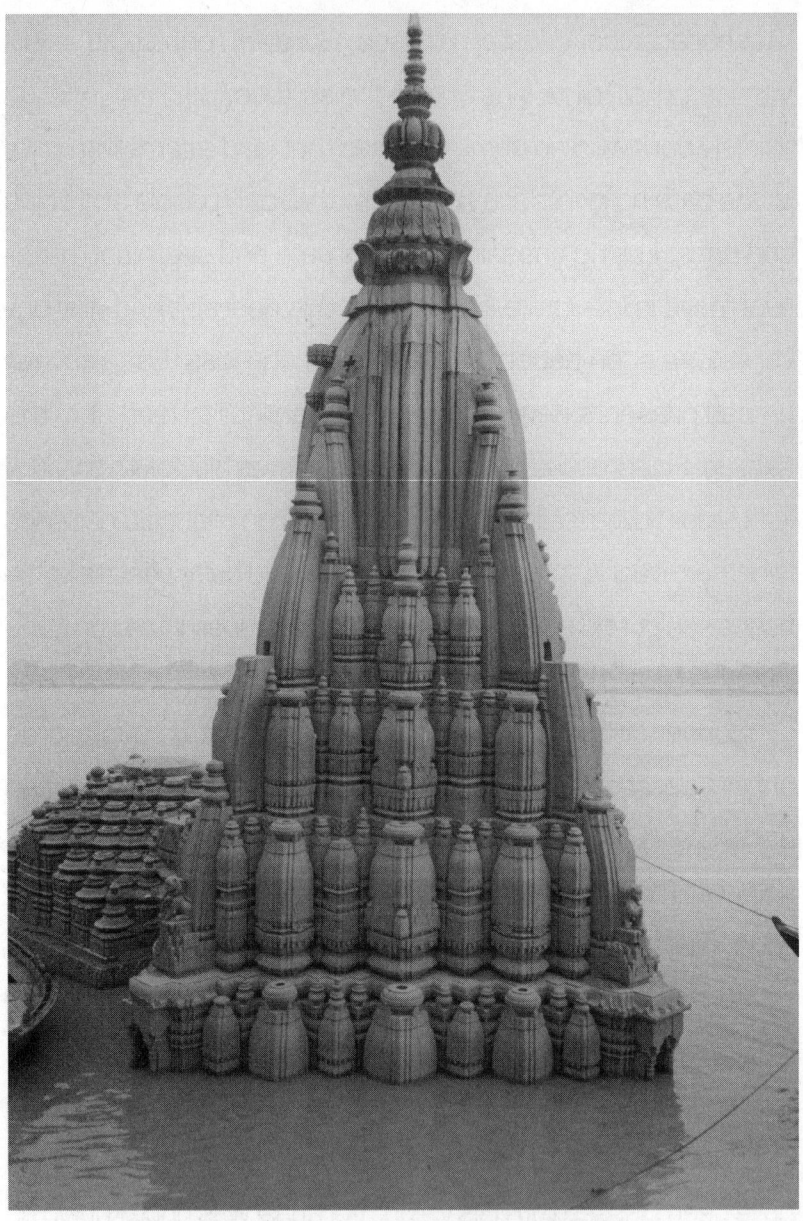

A sunken Siva temple at Manikarnika Ghat.

Varanasi is famous for many things; principally it is famous for death. Death looms large in Kashi and is afforded its proper place—inseparable from life. Sick and aged pilgrims journey from all over India to end their life's pilgrimage here. To die in Varanasi, it is believed, is to be forever liberated from the recurring cycles of birth and death. It is said that Siva himself tenderly whispers the liberating *taraka mantra* into the ear of the dying. Those who cannot make it to Kashi aspire for cremation here; scores of corpses arrive daily for the auspicious privilege of being placed on the pyres at Manikarnika or Harishchandra *ghat*. Carried to their fire by male relatives, the bodies of the dead are held aloft on bamboo stretchers, swathed in cottons or silks, and heaped with flowers. A chant rings out: *Ram Nam Satya Hey! Ram Nam Satya Hey!—God's name is Truth! God's name is Truth!*

The burning *ghats* are at once a sobering, comforting, and awakening experience. At Harischandra *ghat* I sat and observed scenes, which in any other context would have been distressing; but not here, not in this holy place— death is normal, death is sanctifying, death is fine. Death is, after all, just the other side of life. The children of the Doms, the special caste who tend the cremations, played among the smoldering pyres. No one thought this out of place; no one tried to stop them. How refreshing it was to witness no rejection of life and no rejection of death. As I sat, a light covering of ash from the fires softly fell on me like snowflakes, a gentle reminder of what this body will also return to. A young girl took a stick and removed a charred hunk of flesh and bone from a dying fire and hurled it into the Ganga. Only a couple of meters away a woman bathed undisturbed, absorbed in her own rituals of living.

Ascetic and religious traditions of all kinds have long been at home in Varanasi. Its spiritual significance is attested to in the Jain faith by two of their *jinas* or liberators—Suparshva and Parvanatha—taking birth there. Buddha, Mahavira, and Shankaracharya all spent time in Kashi. The Buddha visited in the sixth century B.C.E., coming to the city's deer park to give his first teaching, known as "the turning of the *Wheel of the Law*." Sarnath, as the area is now known, became a great monastic center, and by the seventh century thirty monasteries had developed—a flourishing community of thousands of monks. All of this was later destroyed by the Muslim ruler's armies in the twelfth century.

The city of Siva is also sacred to Vishnu who performed austerities here and bathed in the Ganges. There is a *murti* of Lord Vishnu now housed in the Adi Keshava temple, said to have been created with His own hands. Accordingly, a great lineage of Vaishnavite *bhaktas* arose in Kashi, Ramanuja (1017-1137 C.E.), the great theologian and philosopher of the medieval *bhakta* movement, founded one of the earliest of these orders. He advocated the philosophy of qualified monism involving the worship of a personal God rather than the more

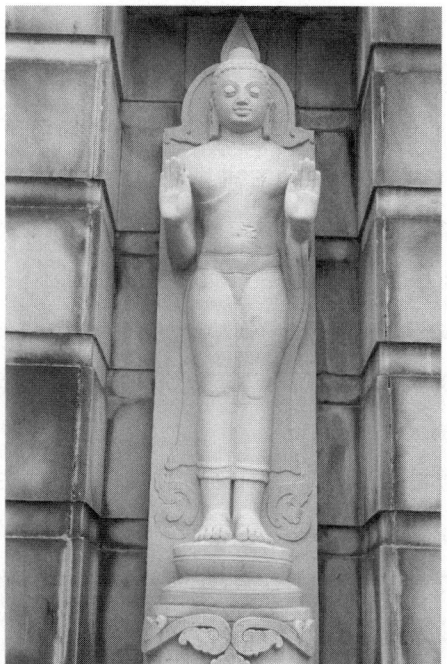

The Buddha at Sarnath's Thai temple.

abstract Brahman. The *sampradayas* that followed him honor that same Vishnu, but in other forms or incarnations.

The acclaimed Ramananda lived in Kashi during the fifteenth century; he was initiated into ascetic life by a disciple belonging to the Shri Sampradaya. Ramananda's devotion was centered on Sri Ramachandra and his beloved consort Sita. Continuous Islamic oppression characterized these times, and Ramananda became a powerful counter force to be reckoned with. He formed an enormously popular *sampradaya,* its success no doubt helped along by the fact that he observed no caste re-strictions.

Ramananda was guru to Kabir, the famous iconoclastic poet and sage. Kabir, always a renegade, took initiation from Ramananda in a somewhat unconventional manner. Early one morning he concealed himself, lying prostrate on the steps of the bathing *ghats* at a spot he knew Ramananda would cross. The great guru duly stepped on Kabir, exclaiming *Ram! Ram!* by way of blessing and as an apology for his carelessness. Kabir took this to be the all-important, difficult to attain moment of *mantra diksa* from the guru.

Kabir's father was Muslim, and throughout life Kabir showed that surrender to God was all that mattered, rather than blind observation of form. He did this by consistently flouting and ridiculing the religious conventions of his day. For the orthodox, Kabir's most confounding demonstration was leaving Varanasi for Magahar as his time of death approached. Magahar was believed to be such an inauspicious place that death there resulted in rebirth as a donkey! Sure enough, Kabir died there leaving the whole matter of liberation from rebirth up to his beloved Ram.

The famous Vaishnavite Acharya Vallabha took the more usual approach, travelling to Kashi in 1532 to take his *maha samadhi.* In front of a gathering of devotees he dove from Hanuman *ghat* into the Ganga and vanished. According to tradition a glowing flame appeared from the waters at that spot.

Another celebrated and saintly poet was Tulsi Das (1543-1623) who translated the *Ramayana* from the Sanskrit of the scholars into the Hindi of the populace. The *Ramcharitmanas*, as it is known, is massively popular throughout central and north India. Mahatma Gandhi considered this the most sublime work on devotion. When Tulsi Das completed the *Ramayana* the pundits of the city were not impressed, fearing it would lose much of its spiritual value couched in the parlance of the masses. They left it overnight at the bottom of a stack of Sanskrit scriptures locked away in the Vishvanath temple. The next morning it had risen mysteriously to the top of the pile, and the pundits, presumably, had to concede it was of some worth! The gleaming white marble Tilsi Das Mandir preserves a pair of the poet's sandals and an original pressing of the *Ramcharitmanas*.

At Asi Ghat I met a gentle Western Sita-Ram *bhakta* by the name of Ram Das. We sat and drank sweet cardamom-infused chai out of clay cups as the sun set over the misty Ganges. A *pujari* came past offering a flame from Ganga *arati*; he pressed a fresh scarlet *kum kum tilak* onto our brows, accepted a few *paise* and moved on. I met Ram Das over the next two days as he happily shared stories of his life in India. At first I had cynically wondered if this dreadlocked *sadhu* was another boring *chillum baba*! However, as he talked of his guru, the magical Devraha Baba, all such concerns dropped away, and a space of openness and receptivity emerged. The repetition of Devraha Baba's name invoked a very definite spiritual presence, a blessing force, and I understood that Ram Das is devoted to his guru.

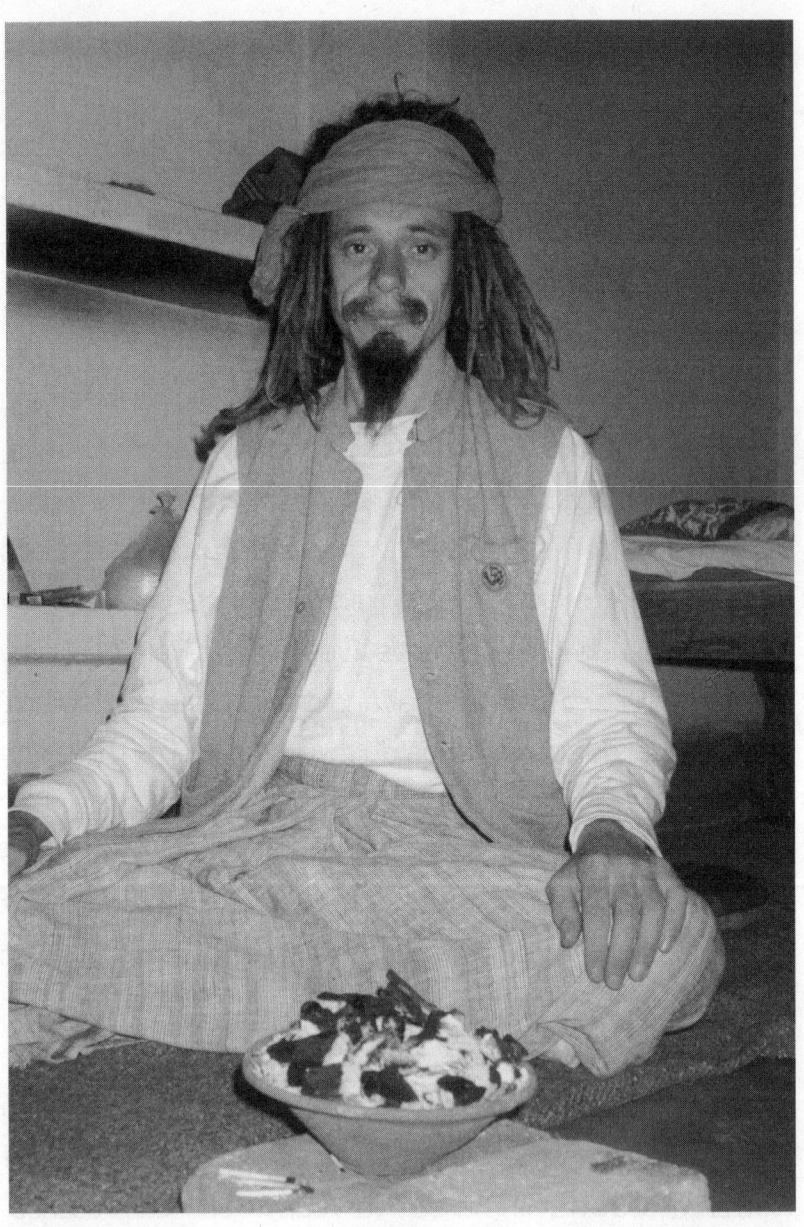

Ram Das

# Ram Das

Before coming to India, when I was in New Zealand, I felt that something was missing. I didn't know what I wanted other than a different lifestyle, and I thought that India might offer that. My oldest sister had already been to India, and when I looked through her photographs there was one of a *sadhu*, though I could not have named him as that. I was intrigued. What is this man? Where is he coming from? I had no idea, but some connection was there.

I arrived in India after four months in Thailand, visiting temples. At Christmas time I headed down to south India. One evening I really started to enquire consciously for the first time. I was very genuinely asking "Who am I?" And, "Who are the people around me?" "What is this life?" I could feel very strongly that I wasn't who I thought I was. Shortly afterwards I went to Madurai to visit the famous temple of Meenakshi and met a Dutch man who had been living as a s*adhu* for ten years. He talked to me and gave *satsang* every evening, but never mentioned the word God. After three days I had to ask him if this was religion. He said "Yes, but not as you've been taught it." Rather, he said that God should be looked on as energy, not as a man sitting in the sky. My body started to tremble in response. I felt it must be like this, and started to become clearer. I could then at least connect with a concept of God.

The friend I had met in Madurai showed me how to travel without money in India, how to move, and hitchhike. One afternoon we were going to a temple in the jungle. Our food had run out, and he told me he would go to a village for rice and *dal*. Just as he was leaving I heard a voice from within saying "Check your money." My bag was two meters away and I was just too lazy to do that. In fact, he never came back. The next day when I looked, all my money was gone. Only my passport remained.

In 1986 I came to the Kumbha Mela in Haridwar, where I first heard the name Devraha Baba. He was living nearby, but I thought, "Why go to see that *baba* two or three kilometers away when there are already one million *babas* here?" At this time I started to have some spiritual experiences with the third eye, which seemed to be a gateway, though I was afraid to go into it. I was scared I would not come back!

The freedom of these *sadhus* interested me—their travelling, and all the external elements—but at that time I did not really know what their lifestyle was about. I met some old *babas* of eighty-five who wanted me to become their *chela,* but I had no feeling to engage this immediately. One day at Nilkant, the spot where Siva is said to have drunk the poison that turned His throat blue, I was walking in the jungle when my sandals broke. I discarded them and thought, "Lord, if you are really there you'll give me another pair." I didn't say this out loud or mention it to anybody, but five minutes later my friend shouted for me that some sandals had come! His stick had gotten stuck under a rock. When he couldn't pull it out, he had to move the rock, and the sandals were underneath. I had put the Lord to the test and He had responded.

I went on various pilgrimages to Badrinath, Kedarnath, Kashmir, and traveled to Thailand when my visa required renewing. There I attended my first meditation retreat, which was excellent. On returning to India I traveled to Sarnath for a second course. There was no imposition of an external teaching, just pure experience. Moving around with *sadhus* I practiced what I'd learnt. At this time I had not met anyone whom I felt was a guru.

Again I had the experience of all my money being stolen. This time it was money my mother had sent (after me being in India for two and a half years) for me to visit the West. I interpreted this as a sign from God that I was supposed to stay in India. I did go back to Australia, via Bangkok, somehow getting there with no money. Coincidences occurred and I felt fully protected, and that there was no problem. Everything came when it was needed. It was too much magic!

On returning to India I met an old friend in Varanasi who showed me a photo of a master from south India. His name was Koti Swami, and he was over one hundred years old at that point. He looked like a Persian Sufi saint. He would sit in temperatures of fifty degrees Celsius, wearing fifteen layers of cloth and a woolen hat. Also I was told he never took a bath. I wanted to meet him, and my friend agreed to take me after first visiting Arunachala mountain in Tiruvannamalai where we could meet another person who knew the way.

When we arrived to meet Koti Swami it was the celebration of Sivarathri and his birthday—an auspicious start. I touched his feet but felt nothing special; he didn't speak English and hardly talked to us, but we sat with him all night.

This swami would never touch any food; his devotees hand-fed him. For the last twelve years he had stayed on the same rooftop without leaving. I walked around this rooftop and found a place to sit at his feet. Devotees kept coming and holding their hands at the swami's mouth; and I didn't know what was going on. My friend Alec was with me, and Koti Swami shook his head in such a way to tell him to do the same thing. Alec placed his hand there and Koti Swami spat out a grape. Alec took it as *prasad*! Another grape came out and Alec gave it to me; more kept coming from his mouth and we shared them between us.

He also gave me a one-rupee coin. All of this was unusual and very auspicious, though we were unaware of that! Koti Swami said to the Indians, "You see, this is how it is done—you share with your brothers. These boys know how to hunt treasure." All this special treatment was forthcoming . . . he even had us sit on his bed (and it's not every day that that's allowed). Next day I was feeling so peaceful, and we took *darshan* again before leaving for Arunachala. This was my first meeting with a master.

At Arunachala I felt completely in tune with myself. Alec had photographs of Devraha Baba and I dreamt I could see him and feel his presence. Alec kept saying I needed a *sadguru* and advised me to take initiation from Devraha Baba. So we went to Vrindivan to ask for *diksa*.

Devraha Baba belonged to a lineage of Sita-Ram *bhaktas;* his teaching was the chanting of God's name. He was a *digambara sadhu,* totally naked or "sky-clad," for as long as anyone knew. And he was said to be three hundred and fifty years old! He preferred to live in a grass hut seven feet above the ground, called a *munch;* he had two such huts on the banks of the Yamuna River. We were told that he would come to people when needed, then withdraw to the jungle for seventy or eighty years, and then come out again.

The last time he appeared was about thirty years ago in Deveriah in northern India, in a time of drought and disease. After some time the villagers realized that their sicknesses were

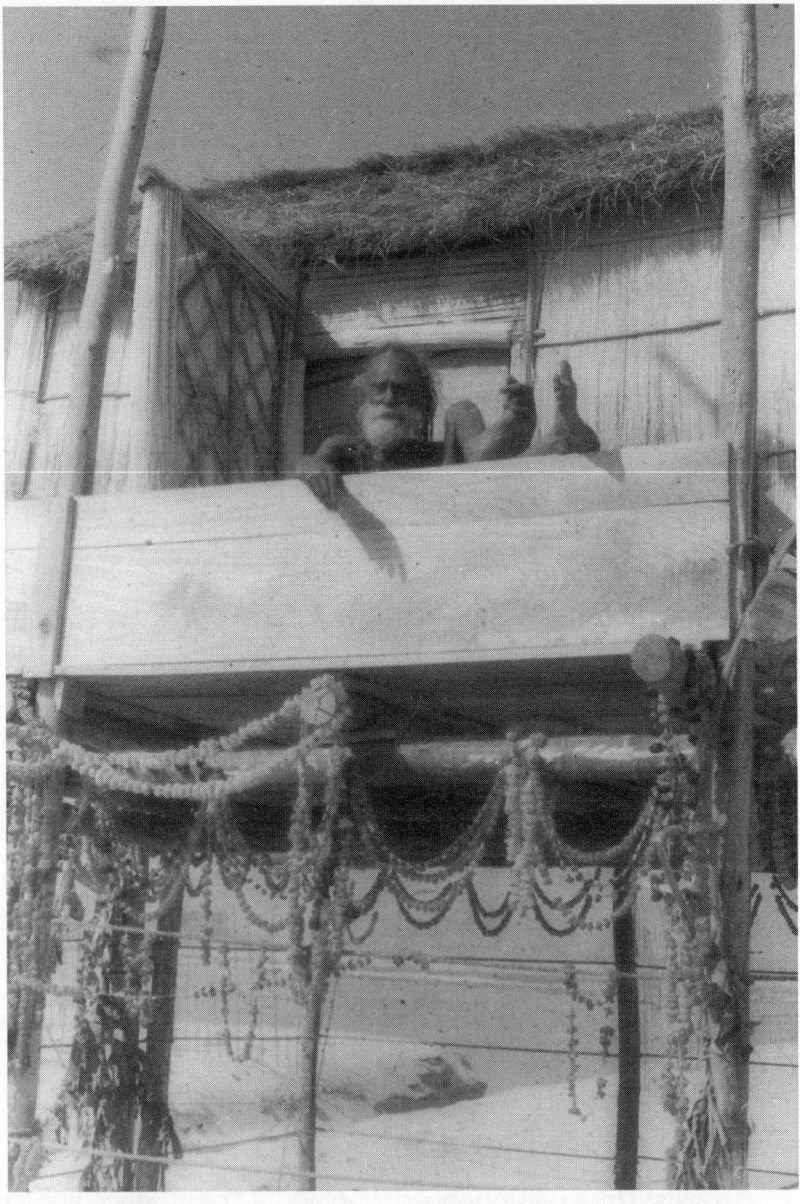

Sri Devraha Baba the Digambara (sky-clad, i.e., naked) *sadhu*, shown here in his preferred dwelling—a grass hut seven feet above the ground, known as a *munch*. Note its location on the sandy banks of a river.

being healed, and that this naked *baba* was someone great. They built him a *munch* and he stayed for thirteen years or so, visiting the Kumbha Melas in Allahbad and Haridwar.

It is recorded that he was present at twelve *mahamelas* in Allahbad. These happen every twelve years, which would make him at least one hundred and forty-four (and he would not have been one year old at his first *mela*!). Baba himself had said, when asked how old he was, "I have some disciples two thousand years old." He also said that he did not take a direct birth, but came directly into the body of a dead boy in a river. He was mostly silent, and kept a distance in his *munch*, which no disciples could enter except his two closest *chelas*. (These became the lineage holders.) When people were invited to come to the side of his *munch*, he would place his foot over the veranda onto their heads to bless them. Indira Gandhi, Rajiv Gandhi, and the king of Nepal also received this same treatment.

The day I came to take initiation I was quite nervous and a little skeptical; in fact, I did not wholly trust him. My friend asked, "This young boy has no guru, can you please initiate him?" Baba simply said yes, and gave me his guru *mantra* and a Vishnu *mantra*.

After initiation I would come every few days to visit. We would sit in a group of a hundred or so, singing *bhajans* around his *munch*. People would come within five or ten meters of the bottom of the *munch*, and he would speak to us from the veranda.

This was the closest I ever got to him. Everyone always left Devraha Baba feeling very happy, with a big smile on his or her face.

At that time I was doing hours of sitting quietly. I asked Baba what *sadhana* I should do, expecting a big list. All he said was to chant the *mantra* and he would do the rest; I received no other instruction. I've noticed that many great masters operate in this way. He also gave me the name Ram Das.

We talked about the future and what we should do. He told us the world was going to go through a difficult period, and that we should find a group of people, some land, and stay there. We were already looking to buy land, but couldn't find anything suitable, so we left Vrindivan and went to Haridwar. While we were in Haridwar, much to our surprise Devraha Baba left his body. It had only been three months since I'd met him.

I left India to stay in Australia for six months, but six months turned into three and a half years of working in Sydney. Spiritually I felt I was going nowhere and that it was time to go back to India. Even after four years of initiation I did not understand who Devraha Baba was.

I came back to India expecting to find Alec who had taken me to Baba and Koti Swami originally. Alec had died. I wanted to visit Koti Swami again, but also I found out that he had left his body too. It was upsetting; they had all died. I decided to go to Vrindivan to Devraha Baba's *samadhi* site.

An ashram was under construction and Baba's closest *chelas,* Dev Das and Ram Sawak Das were present. Actually, they did not remember me, and were surprised when I told them my name. I developed a relationship with these two: they gave *satsang* and stressed the importance of the *mantra* repetition. They kept telling me about Baba's grace, and that he was still there; but I remained sceptical.

The next Kumbha Mela came, and after some time I was taken to meet another guru. I asked him about the masters, and if they were still here helping after they had left the body. He said, "Yes, whether you know it or not they are still here and helping us very much."

At the '95 *mela*, the day before the parade started, Baba's photo winked at me twice during *arati.* I knew he was still here—I could understand that. The next day we paraded through the Kumbha Mela with a life-sized painting of Baba on a carriage drawn by white horses. The carriage was fully decorated with orange and yellow chrysanthemums, even the spokes of the wheels were covered. Dev Das and Ram Sewak Das sat on either side of Baba's image. We followed behind, singing *bhajans;* thousands of people came for blessings. Afterwards, at the makeshift ashram, we sat singing around the *dhuni* fire. I felt a vibration at the *Ajna chakra*—very strong. It felt that this energy penetrated the whole Universe. I could approach it very humbly and was moved to say internally, "Devraha Baba, I humbly touch your feet." Instantly I was completely blinded with an explosion of white light. Later, again Baba's photo came to life and Baba said to me, internally, "You are blessed." I asked what I should do now and he told me, "Be yourself."

Since that time I have not left India, although I've traveled a little to pilgrimage places and continue to chant my *mantra* every day. Looking back I realize that the source of all my protection in life is Devraha Baba. He is always there with me. For the foreseeable future I will remain in India, but it may be that I will return to the West.

Baba was asked, "What about these foreigners who are coming; what is their relationship to you and can they understand also?" He replied, "Yes, they were my disciples in their last life and I helped them find good parents in the West so they can serve from there. If they do the correct *sadhana* they will get it." First we have to learn here and in the future we will be back in our respective places to serve him. All I want to do in my life is to serve him. I surrender to him.

Devraha Baba took *samadhi* on the day of Yogini Ekadasi in June 1990.

He was sitting in full lotus position. Devotees present said his feet started to get cold, and then his legs; the heat in his body was shifting upwards. A dark heavy line appeared on the forehead, and consciousness left through the crown. His last message to the world was the following:

Lord Brahma lives on the cow's back. Within the cows' neck resides Vishnu in invisible form. Within the cow's mouth, Lord Siva. Within the cow's body-hair reside all Gods and Hermits. In her full form, eight parts, the Goddess of Wealth.

Mother Lakshmi is in the cow's dung. The cow's importance is very big: all Gods are walking where the cow roams. If you want to re-establish Indian values then protect the cows. Hindus, Muslims, Christians, Parsis, Jewish and everyone should stand to save the cow. I tell you very lovingly in this moment India's dirtiness and the killing of cows must be stopped: on this there is no compromise.

# 5

Swami Vijayananda's name had been given to me in Varanasi by a kind-hearted Western *sadhu* known as Govinda. (The god Krishna was known as Govinda during his buoyant adolescence, when mischief and lighthearted fun were his calling cards.) True to his name, Govinda led me on a playful adventure; I knew he had a wonderful story to tell, but I also knew he had no intention of telling it! Over several days we met by the *ghats* and proceeded to various events (*bhajans* at a friend's home, a classical music recital), me with my notepad and pen ever ready, and he occasionally gesturing "Maybe later." We both enjoyed this game, and Govinda played it right up until our last moments together when he finally gave me details of Swami Vijayananda, and other useful contacts.

With Govinda one entered a playful dance: when I became overly serious and anxious about the project, he would glance over at me with sparkling, gently-mocking eyes. That look was disarming, leaving me open to whatever *lila* was arising in that moment.

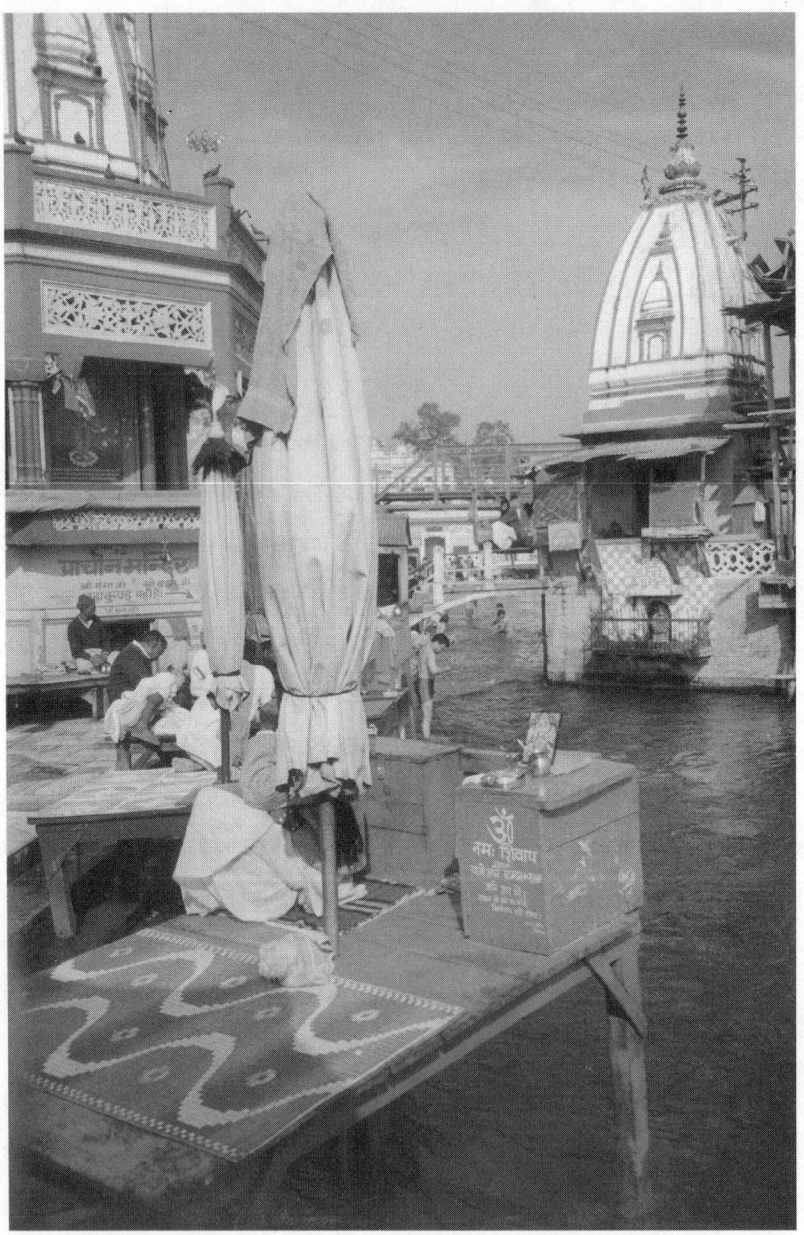

Amongst the temples, shrines, pundits and pilgrims at the Hari ki Pauri *ghat*, Haridwar.

The train journey from Kashi to Haridwar is beautiful, sweeping through peaceful rural landscapes and dusty, sleepy villages. The furious intensity of Varanasi soon fades, and the pace of life relaxes into a more natural rhythm. Minarets of crumbling mosques punctuate the skyline in the dusky evening light, and the sight of bullock carts plowing open fields is strangely soothing.

Temperatures plummeted as the train headed further north, and a chilling fog appeared as night descended. It was the coldest winter India had endured for twenty years. Unprepared, I put on every single piece of thin cotton clothing in my possession and curled up into a ball in a rather unsuccessful attempt to keep warm—it was a long night!

Alighting from Haridwar station, the first sight that confronts you is a huge, bland, pastel blue head of Siva, complete with a fountain of Ganges water spouting from his locks. A flash of anger arose in me. "This is one of the holiest towns in all of India! What can they be thinking of, desecrating it with sacrilegious trash?" Yet, to appreciate India one needs to be able to read such symbols—as tawdry as the artistry may be, they can still be utilized as profound reminders of the Absolute.

Haridwar is a bustling town with something of the air of a Western seaside resort; the many shops and stalls do a brisk trade in religious memorabilia. Pilgrims flock to take a purifying dip in the icy Ganges, particularly at Har Ki Pairi *ghat*, which marks the exact spot where the holy river leaves the mountains and enters the plains. The bridge across the Ganga here is a highly lucrative spot for beggars, of which there are many. They are well organized, and have overlords who effectively "employ" them. (More sinister is that once one has entered a begging circle, one may be barred from leaving it.) During festivals and particularly at the Kumbha Mela, competition over this bridge location becomes fierce, with rival groups aggressively clashing over which has the right to beg there. One interviewee told me of watching private buses arrive in the pre-dawn hours to drop the beggars off, and returning late at night to pick them up again. The governmental authorities, embarrassed by the image India's hordes of beggars project onto their "modern" society, have started widespread, subsidized re-education and work-placement schemes. They have met with only partial success; many prefer the life of begging, seeing it as a legitimate and traditional way of earning their livelihood.

Haridwar *ghats* are unusually clean, the many shrines freshly painted in glossy white and glaring vermilion. If one had been hoping for the ambience of the ancient, it is not to be found here. Pundits and priests abound, tending to the needs of pilgrims, and ready to perform all kinds of rituals for a few *rupees*. There are thousands of *sadhus* and *sannyasins* in Haridwar, but most of them remain out of sight, behind the walls of the many large, purposely-built ashrams.

The ashram of Sri Anandamayee Ma (1896-1982), the widely revered woman mystic, is a cool and tranquil retreat from

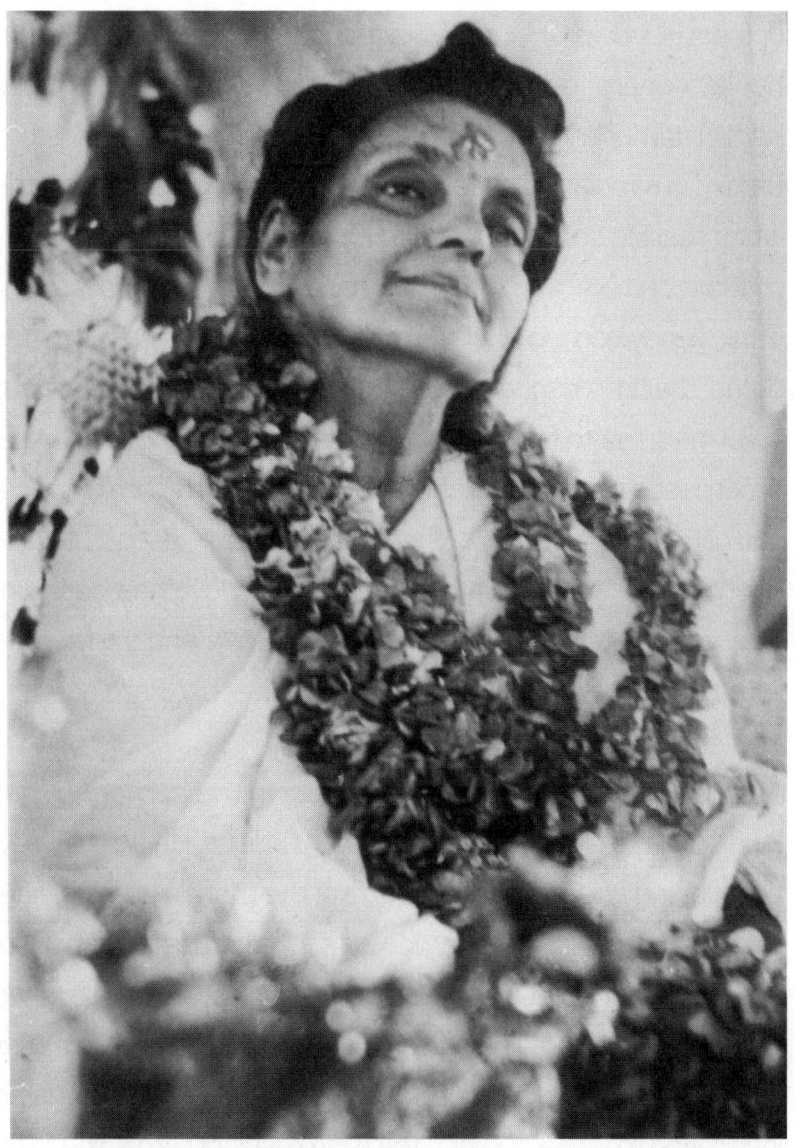

Sri Anandamayee Ma.

uptown Haridwar. Here the illustrious saint spent much time in her later years: her room is still kept untouched as a shrine to her remembrance. The whole atmosphere of the ashram is bathed in a radiant silence, which seems to focalize around the white marble *samadhi* temple. *Puja* is performed here every morning and evening by specially trained young *brahmacharyas*. Thick, heady incense swirls through the air; songs of praise softly drone; the *brahmacharyas* use great white horsetail whisks with silver handles to fan the marigold-adorned tomb. The ritual progresses slowly and elaborately, a moving rhythmic invocation of Sri Ma's blessing. When the ceremony reaches its crescendo one feels that a force of light and love has been unleashed. The photographs and *murti* of Sri Anandamayee Ma in the adjacent rooms are very much alive, her gaze ecstatic and tender.

Outside in an open courtyard facing the *samadhi* I met Swami Vijayananda in the fading evening light. He sits here every evening after the *puja*, on one of the marble steps, and a mat is rolled out for anyone who would like his association. Usually it is only a handful. Swami Vijayananda struck me as being extremely soft and alert. This elderly *sannyasin* smiled often, revealing the light that seemed to glow inside him. It was an inspiration to witness in him the living result of remaining faithful to the guru's instruction over a lifetime. Swami Vijayananda's simple and unassuming manner extended toward his attitude to *sannyas*, which did not seem to matter to him one way or another; he just accepted what Sri Anandamayee Ma offered.

The last time we met was on a quiet cold Christmas Eve. Swami Vijayananda distributed chocolates as *prasad* to the three or four of us gathered around him. My fellow seekers drifted away, and I remained alone with him in the ultramarine night. An air of mystery and wonder arose in me, appropriate to that special time of year and, as I looked into Swami Vijayananda's face, I knew I was looking at someone who was at home in the depth of that mystery, that silent, spacious night.

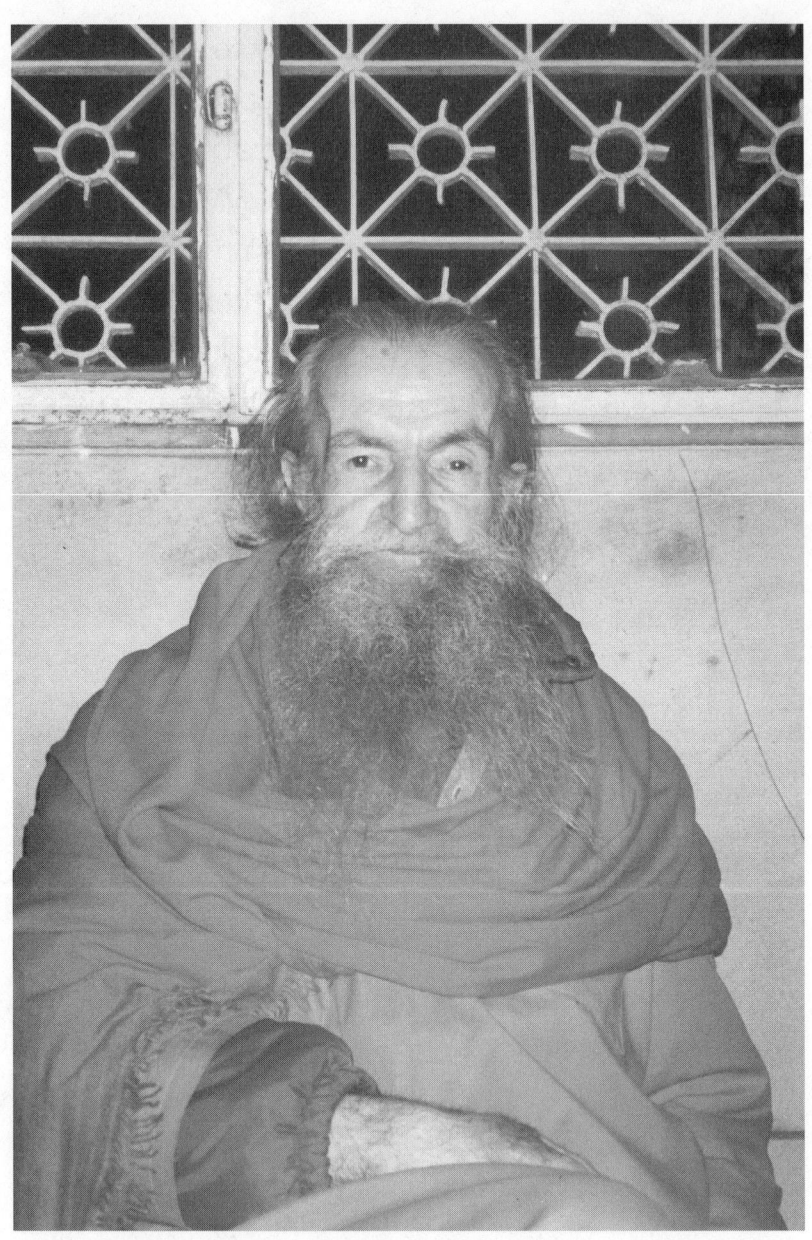

Swami Vijayanada

# Swami Vijayananda

Despite a very religious childhood I became an atheist as I grew up. Nonetheless, I was impressed when I read Vivekananda's *Raja Yoga*, his first book on yoga. I was a doctor, a GP, in a small town in France for eight years, during which time I began to be more and more interested in Theravada Buddhism and Vedanta. I provisionally placed a substitute in charge of my medical practice and left France in quest of spiritual guidance in this country, India, which since time immemorial has illumined the world. It was the second of February 1951, at about six o'clock in the evening, when I first saw my guru.

I had landed in Buddhist Ceylon and proceeded along the east coast of India, arriving in Benares. I was tired, disappointed, and almost convinced that my journey had been in vain. I was determined to return to France, and had already reserved a berth on the *Marseillaise*, which was to sail from Colombo on February 21st. I had come searching for a guru, not just a teacher—one of those great beings who can, by their mere presence, awaken in us the inner power which makes real *sadhana* possible. I knew nothing about Sri Ma Anandamayee. A friend I met had advised me to visit her ashram nested on the banks of the Ganges. I noted her name among other things worthwhile to be seen in Benares, having already lost hope of finding the sage I was looking for.

I entered her ashram through a small door in a narrow lane, and found myself in a vast majestic ashram overlooking the Ganges, with a breathtaking view along the *ghats*. My first idea was to simply have a look and go away, but Sri Ma was just coming out of one of the buildings and my companion introduced me to her. They were talking in Bengali and he told me "Ma says you are good." She was fifty-five, looking younger than her age, still beautiful. At that moment I did not notice her beauty, it was only later that I became aware of it. I still see her, focusing her eyes on me with that strange gaze that seemed to embrace my whole destiny. I had nothing to ask her. She seemed to divine thought. It was she who put the questions—clear, precise, going straight to the heart of things, raising the exact points that interested me. But her words were only a play on the surface. My first impression was of surprise. I had expected to see an old lady with white hair.

The real "happening" was inside of me. It was like somebody throwing a lighted match in gunpowder. You know something extraordinary is going to happen, although it does not happen at that very moment. In that moment I felt something strange, which I could not define. But indeed, a few hours later, after I had gone to my hotel, the explosion occurred—a feeling of unearthly joy and happiness. "I have found the guru I was looking for!" There was no shadow of doubt about that in my mind.

What gave me this conviction? People will call it love. But the English word is misleading for this wonderful relationship between guru and disciple. The guru is not only dearer than a mother, a father, or a friend; all the shades of love and veneration are contained in this relationship. Any worldly love, however pure and sublimated it may be, ends in disillusion and sorrow. But the love of the guru purifies the mind and liberates us from worldly attachment. It is like a flawless mirror, which reflects our own higher self and leads to the eternal source of peace and happiness, which is inside ourselves.

As if by a strange alchemy, my entire potentiality for affection, all that one can love and admire in the world, had been transferred to Sri Ma Anandamayee. But at the same time, this love became so pure, so sublimated, that it merged into, and greatly intensified, the call for the Absolute that I always felt. All worldly attachment lost its attraction and the spiritual ascent became easier. In one single person, all that one can love, respect, admire, and adore became identified with the *Sadguru*, the Lord. It is through this love that one can renounce, all of a sudden, the comforts of a luxurious life and devote oneself entirely to the search for the Supreme. It is through this love that one gets the strength to conquer *kama*, *krodha* and *lobha*—lust, anger and greediness.

To sit at Ma's holy feet was not only a source of peace and bliss, it was also a most powerful *sadhana*. Her very presence purified the mind, loosening age-long fetters. Without telling a word she could open the way of the *nadis,* granting one, in a few minutes, what would have taken many years of strenuous *sadhana*.

My relationship with Ma was that with a guru , but she was much more than this. She was doubtlessly a Divine Being. Sri Ma had told us that she had not come to Earth as a result of *prarabdha karma,* and that in fact she had had no previous births. Was she an *avatar*? Or a perfect sage who had come down to help humanity? Much has been written or speculated about it. What is certain is that the lady we called Sri Anandamayee Ma was a vehicle for an immense power of infinite love.

At the beginning, for nineteen months I was constantly with her, except for one day. We often traveled together in the same train compartment or in the same car. At the beginning, when we were in the same compartment at night I had the habit of occupying the upper berth, above Ma. But once I understood better who she was, I used to lie down on the floor. We had a very simple relationship—we used to eat together. But, after some pundits remarked that this contravened the rules, we discontinued the practice. In the initial years I did not speak Hindi, and my communication with Ma was always silent. I asked her questions and received her replies all within myself. I also learnt through direct observation.

The first few times I had to leave Ma for a long period were terrible. One day during one of these difficult periods I wrote to her, half-jokingly, "Ma this is very hard. Can't you do the *sadhana* in my place?" She replied, "A *sadhaka* should first of all learn patience. With the help of patience the *sadhaka* should enter within his self, and Realization will become his."

I never returned to the West. The first eighteen months were spent constantly in her company, and then I stayed at the Benares ashram on the banks of the Ganges for eight years. In 1956 I was doing intense *tapasaya* in Vindichal, not far from Benares. I went to see Ma, and we were three or four on the ashram terrace. Ma saw the dark brown robe I was wearing. It was the only one I had and it was a bit torn at the back, but I hadn't noticed it. She started laughing and tore it completely, while I was doing *pranam* to her. I told her "Ma, you gave me *sannyas!*" and she smiled. Before I received the ochre clothes I was always careful not to use a color that resembled it. However, one day after washing it, my brown robe came out sort of orange. I asked Ma if it was okay, and she said, "It is the *gerua*" (that is to say, the ochre color that is reserved for *sannyasins*) which is inside that is coming out. In 1976, for her eightieth birthday, she gave me some cloth to make a complete ochre robe. By myself, I would never have taken the ochre robe, and did not in fact take the vows of a *sannyasi*, because I wanted to remain free. Besides, I think that these vows are part of those typically Hindu customs, which perhaps Westerners can drop. Ma also gave me this name.

As time progressed our relationship became more impersonal, though just as intense. I had noticed that when my practice was sound, Ma used to be cold and distant, but when practice was not going so well she was warm and gentle.

Meditation ultimately leads to a realization of the impersonal, but a personal relationship helps a great deal in achieving that stage.

At one point I wanted to leave Ma and return to France. She was very gentle and said: "If you are fed up with seeing this face, you may go away!" I stayed on.

I was at that time very attached to Ma's physical form, I must have had need of this attachment. But Ma liberated me from it. When a real guru creates an attachment for a specific reason, they also have the power to liberate you from it. For some years I could distinguish between the interior impulses that came from myself and those that came from Ma. Afterwards I could not distinguish anymore. Ma had a great deal of energy. When she walked, one had to run to keep up with her. When she swam, she swam like a fish. But at the end, before leaving her body, she had difficulty moving from one place to another and had to be moved in a wheelchair. Once at Benares I had a rat bite, which after some days had become infected. I tried not to let Ma see it, but a *sadhu* denounced me. Once she looked at it, the infection practically disappeared within twenty-four hours. Perhaps it was because of her disciples that Ma used to be ill so often. That may be the reason why Vivekananda, who did not protect himself from his followers and hardly took any care of his physical health, died young.

After spending some years in the Himalayas doing solitary practice, I came to Ma's Haridwar ashram at her request. This was in 1975, and I could see her rather frequently until she left her body in 1982. I found that with age she became very serious, very "wise." I asked her, "Ma, why aren't you like before? Have you changed?" She answered, "I haven't changed, but it is this body which has grown old." Toward the end of her life where so many people came to see her she was obliged to select the serious spiritual seekers from among the crowd that also contained the merely curious.

At her *samadhi* there is always a lot of activity, and people say they sense her presence. Basically, Ma had already become identified with the Absolute before she left her physical body. Now that she has left her body, identification with the Absolute is the only state she is in. Whether she has left any traces, subtle or otherwise, is a very delicate question. The teachings of Sri Anandamayee Ma can be summarized with one sentence she often repeated: "To find Bhagavan (God) is to find your own self. And to discover your own self is to find Bhagavan." That is to say, if you start your quest for the Divine by the path of devotion, you will end by finding that this Divine resides in your own heart, and that it is of the same nature as the omnipresent. If you start the quest with "Who am I?"—which is the path of knowledge—the Divine will reveal itself as being your true nature.

To reach this knowledge there are numerous paths and that is what we call a *sadhana*. Ma used to guide each and everyone on the path that was best suited to him or her. She did not impose a particular line of *sadhana*. But the first goal was the discovery of the fact that the individual soul is no different from the Divine omnipresent. And that is the essence of Vedanta.

Beginners who are seeking a spiritual master can go from one sage to another just to assess the situation. But when you become a real disciple of a real guru you become a part of his body and you can never leave him. It would be a diminishing of energy to go like a butterfly from one to the other simply to see. Indians understand that very well, but Westerners have difficulty with it. If a guru does not transmit power to his disciples he is not a guru. It's not very difficult to become a guru in India, you know. One must have a gift of the gab, a head for business, and—this is important—an orange robe, if possible, and a beautiful graying or white beard like mine!

In the forty-five years during which I've seen Westerners come to India in search of God, I've noticed defects in their approach. Firstly they have very strong egos. Secondly, they want immediate results; they do not have the patience to do long sustained *sadhanas*. Thirdly, as soon as they have had two or three spiritual experiences they want to open centers and start teaching. Generally the Westerners are intellectuals who believe one can solve all religious and philosophical problems through discussions on the concepts. In the person raised in traditional Eastern culture this attitude seems strange. In the spiritual and philosophical teachings *he* receives, he sees scientific truths that he can trust for the reason that they have been experienced by millions of people before him. His only task is to verify and realize them through his own experience. Imagine that you went to a research chemist and asked him, "What would've happened if Lavoisier had made a mistake in the enunciation of his laws?" He would look at you in amazement and doubtlessly reply: "Don't ask me useless questions! Just tell me what you want me to produce for you."

But at their own level, people in the world are right when they say that religion is a load of rubbish, for they do not feel anything when they meditate; and the *sadhakas* are right when they say that the world is rubbish, because they do not feel anything when thinking and looking at worldly pleasures.

There are differences between the East and West in their approach to the Absolute. First, there is a duality between God and the creature, which is fundamental in the West, and which is much attenuated in the East. For instance, every Hindu knows that God is inside him, and that he is not different from his innermost Self. On the other hand, in the West, people are influenced by the Greek philosophy, and they believe they can reach the Absolute by discussion. In India this is secondary. Here it is acknowledged that some sages have reached the Absolute and can give practical means to achieve it, and that's all.

One reason for the relative absence of sages in the West is that Westerners do not have the capacity of spontaneous trust, which could enable them to blossom. This is why Jesus could not perform miracles in Nazareth. People could not trust him as a sage or a Divine Incarnation because they only projected an ordinary man—their former neighbor—on him. Looking for a Christian Vedanta is somehow an impossibility, because Christianity is dualistic and Vedanta is non-dualistic. However, Ramana Maharshi was right when he advised Christians to meditate on "I am who I am." This definition of God by Himself is pure Vedanta. The very word *Yahweh* contains past, present, and future. From another point of view, the Western system has its advantages as well: frankly dualistic for the people, with a non-dualistic tendency for mystics. In any case, a mystic who has a true realization, whatever path he may follow, cannot speak of it. Vedanta is not a description of reality: it is simply a path to reach it. Human beings need to understand that there is only one religion, that of man. The various religions are merely sects, and these sects create wars.

There have been schools in India—Theravada Buddhism, Vijnanavada, and a few late Vedantic schools as well—that used to teach the notion of the complete unreality of the world. This attitude can be useful for some time for the *sadhaka* to develop a spirit of detachment, but this is not the position of Mahayana Buddhism, which believes that the world (samsara) and nirvana are one. Neither is the case in the path I follow, Vedanta, which states that the world is real since it is pure consciousness. As a substance, it is as real as water, but as a movement it is as transitory as the wave; but even there, it cannot be said that it is completely unreal, we just don't understand where its reality lies. It is said in the Katha Upanishad: "What is here is over there, what is over there is here; he who sees a difference goes from death to death."

The seclusion of the yogi is not an escape from the world. In the mind of the yogi the seclusion is always temporary—it is the time taken for attaining a certain level of consciousness. After that he returns to the world. For him, the people of the world are really escaping. They are escaping from themselves, trying to lose themselves in activism, women, and politics. They are avoiding the main questions, like, What is the origin of suffering?, How can it be cured?, What is the meaning of life? The yogi faces these questions and faces himself.

I am a very ordinary man. However, I do not have negative emotions: no anger, no sexual desire, which is so difficult to master, no attachments. Of course, during meditation I have bliss, but to maintain it permanently in daily life is much more difficult. That corresponds to the summit of spiritual evolution, sahaja samadhi, which is spontaneous samadhi.

# 6

Penny Ma is an enigmatic figure, a sadhu with a strong energy and feisty manner; my mind would come to a halt in her company, as one had no idea what was coming next. At once encouraging and scornful of this project, she told me she had no desire to participate in it, only to spend the next three days generously sharing the more significant events in her remarkable life story.

Penny Ma has that Indian talent for great storytelling: it was hard to keep a linear sense of events as we were sidetracked by frequent, fascinating anecdotes about life in India and her meetings with various masters. For instance: Penny Ma and her husband of the time came to Haridwar to meet Sri Anandamayee Ma. Conscious of the fact that they were visiting a great saint, beautiful gifts had been prepared as an offering. When they entered the *darshan* hall, Sri Anandamayee Ma immediately spotted them and started to quiver and cower under her sari, covering her face as though the sight of them was too much to bear. They came forward and placed their offering of *prasad* on the stage, by Sri Ma's feet. Cringing still further away on their approach, Sri Ma, with the minimum of contact possible, deftly kicked the offerings off the platform, quickly retracting her foot to safety. Sri Ma continued to keep herself covered, fearfully peeking out, occasionally, to see if these sources of pollution were still around! Ashram staff threw the presents out onto the road, and Penny Ma left with her suitably shocked husband.

In the early hours of the next morning Penny Ma was awakened by a vision of Sri Anandamayee Ma saying, "Come, now!" Feeling that what she was doing was insane, she nevertheless got onto her bicycle and rode the fair distance to Sri Ma's ashram at top speed. It was about three-thirty in the morning, and strangely the ashram gates were not locked.

Not knowing where she was going, Penny Ma felt guided to a particular room. Opening the door she found Sri Anandamayee Ma sitting up in bed, waiting for her. Sri Ma said, "You have come," and took Penny into her arms. It was an experience of being utterly loved and affirmed by the Divine. Sri Ma's female attendants, returning to the room from their early morning baths, were outraged to see this foreign intruder in the arms of their beloved guru. They shrieked in horror, roughly dragged Penny Ma out of the room, and threw her out of the ashram. During this commotion, Sri Ma's eyes did not leave those of Penny Ma and registered tender concern, though she remained silent.

Outside the ashram, Penny Ma walked down the street, still

lost in the intimate reverie of Ma's embrace, when those same ladies came running after her and begged her to return to the ashram. Penny Ma was not interested, feeling she had received everything and needed nothing. However, Sri Ma must have given a stiff ultimatum, as the ladies were not taking no for an answer. Seeing that their pleading was to no avail, they turned to force and, in a comic reversal of the earlier scene, dragged her back to the ashram. Here, Sri Ma gave Penny *prasad* to seal the morning's magical events.

We spoke on the sunny terrace of her small and attractive ashram, overlooking the turquoise calm of the Ganges, and interrupted now and then by the appearance of one of her playful dogs. Penny Ma loves dogs and appreciates their qualities of innocent affection and obedience. As a quivering "sausage" dog leapt onto my lap, Ma quoted guru Nanak, "Be God's dog: be a dog for God." She pointed out that this meant surrender—the single biggest difficulty for Western seekers on the path. I had to wonder what teaching lessons were to be garnered from the star-shelled tortoise in the corner of the room.

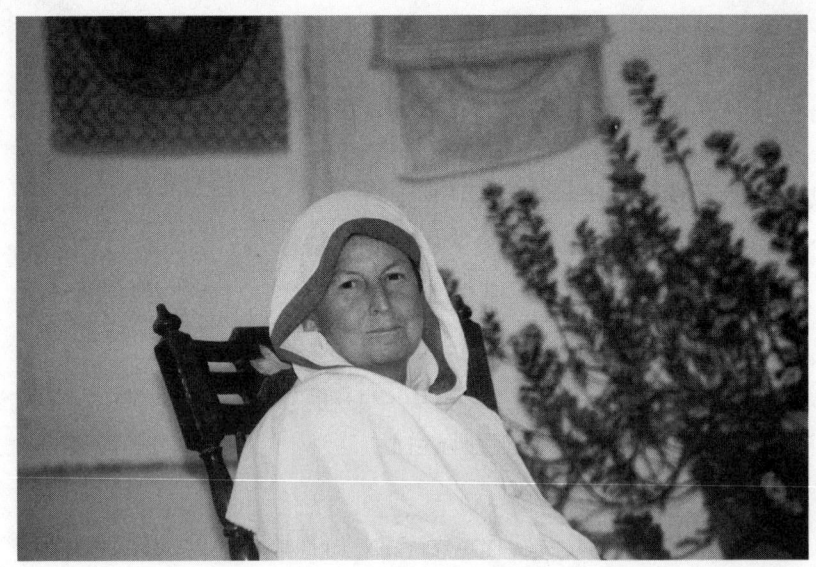

The *sadhini* Penny Ma

# Penny Ma

*How do you get into spiritual life?* I didn't, it happened to me.
I was a person not the least interested in the spiritual, certainly
not a seeker. I was a housewife, into art and performing songs
in coffee shops in Toronto in the 1950s. One day I was walking
with my husband, shopping, and I saw someone buying a chicken
in the market. Suddenly I was struck with an overpowering feeling of revulsion—I felt it was wrong. I decided to never eat meat
again. It was 1957, so this was a little unusual then.

I met my guru, my first guru, around this time, though I did
not even know what a guru was then. My guru found me—I was
not looking, though I had managed to marry the son of one of
his chief devotees, without knowing it. Experiences of various
sorts started to happen and I made some dramatic decisions.
I got up one morning and left the whole of my former life behind;
I never spoke to my friends or husband again after this point. I
got in my car, left everything and, to my great surprise, fell at
my guru's feet and cried. He said, "It's enough. Now you can

rest; you can stop." It took twenty years to know what he was really talking about.

I had made a vow not to speak to any of my former friends, and did not want to speak to my parents again, either. This is the proof of *samskaras;* a normal person does not make such a decision and have the power to keep it. My family had me put in jail and wanted to have me committed to a mental institution, but the vow was so complete that when they looked into my eyes they backed off and stopped pursuing me. It would never have worked if I was desperately grappling with this—but I wasn't; I just completely changed overnight. I was the only child, so the drama lasted for a few months. However, my guru intervened and said it was wrong not to speak to my mother, so I spoke then, reluctantly, only to my parents, though I never went into their house again. We met just occasionally in restaurants and public places. I would look at former friends and know that what I was doing was impossible and strange, yet ninety percent of me was unaffected. I did not recognize people from before anymore.

My guru refused to let me quit my job, yet still I was not speaking to anyone I had previously known. Also, I had made a vow not to touch money. Nonetheless, I remained in my job at the library in Toronto for nine years and did not touch money for that time, though it was rather complicated. I was on fire with energy. People at work became frightened of me and would keep quiet when I came into the room. But they never sacked me.

I lived with my guru for nine years and he never once gave me a bed. I just had to bed down wherever I was—like an animal. He never paid the slightest attention to what my condition was. Once, at three A.M. during one of the worst winters Canada had experienced for years, he kicked me awake and said, "Have you seen the snow outside? We're going to get snowed in! I need my tractor. Go and get it." The tractor was eighty miles away, in his summer camp. But, you see, you jump up and devour such opportunities because this is how you learn. Everything the guru throws at you, you should devour—the bigger the better; the more you have to eat. You should be insatiable for that. For four years, every time I went to the toilet (or should I say, practically every time,) my guru would come and bang on the door saying that he had to go and I had to get out.

This was the only personal space left to me and he took it away. He destroyed my sense of having a right to a good night's sleep, or a right to go to the toilet. If you serve a guru you suspend all such rights.

The vows went on. I took a vow not to sleep for six months, and nothing detrimental happened to my health.

In 1964 I came to India with my guru and his group. It was no spiritual whammy, but really bewildering and frightening, with the notable exception that I really loved Haridwar and Har Ki Pairi. After that I went back and forth to India three or four times, and every time I returned to the West I regretted it. But when I was in India I thought it was awful and that I really hated it. I went to the Kumbha Mela in 1971 intending to stay for a month, but left after seven days, rushing back in tears. Yet, within two weeks I was thinking, why in God's name did I leave that place?

Finally I chose India for good, in 1975, and moved here with my second husband. The first year was a trial of fire; I feel this was done directly by God as I had made a vow not to leave India. My husband became very ill in Haridwar, and circumstances were pretty devastating. We had, by this point, no money—not a single rupee. He entered into a coma, and it was hell—he was dying in front of my eyes. I called for an ambulance that never came, and at midnight got him into a taxi, which broke down! I was left on the road with my husband in this condition. Finally, the taxi driver came back with a friend and we got him to hospital. When we got there the entire medical staff was waiting up for us. He stayed for two months; we were given a private air-conditioned room. People visited us everyday, brought us fruit and raised money for us. We became local heroes. It was hard to go back to our normal room afterwards.

While my husband had been in hospital, I had a biopsy, and later the result came back. I was simply and heartlessly told that I had breast cancer. They gave me a thirty percent chance of survival. I went into the fetal position and wept—I was finished off. Still, I was thrown into awareness of the Now (even then, even there—right there as I lay in the fetal position), and that awareness has never left me. I can't tell you how wonderful that is. All these experiences just filled me with determination, made me feel more courageous, more filled with bliss, closer to God.

Back in Delhi, we were plunged back into the same circumstances of poverty and extreme illness. I decided to have the cancer operation in India, and the doctors were stunned—I was the first Westerner to have that operation in Delhi. When I went to the hospital there were six doctors having tea, and among them happened to be the top breast cancer surgeon in Asia who had been giving a seminar. He was flying to Malaysia the next day. When he heard about me he cancelled the flight and performed the operation himself. A few weeks later he died of a heart attack. They pickled my breast and use it today in a teaching hospital.

I had no money while all this was going on, yet we were given VIP treatment. So many doctors visited us, and their wives sent perfume and homemade cookies. Masses of flowers arrived every day. My husband said, "Gosh, I hope we don't get a bill at the end of all this." Anyway, there were more operations to come, radiotherapy, and no funds for a proper diet to recover. Then I developed appendicitis and it looked like I might die. Still, I just clung on by my fingernails thinking that it would be better here in India; that God was doing everything. Because I was looked after in these circumstances, I can now look back and trust God and say, "Okay, whatever You want."

We went to stay at my first guru's ashram in north India,

which happened to be next door to the ashram of Chandra Swami, who a friend of ours had met many times. Chandra Swami's books had been given to us, but we were dead set against meeting him because we wanted to just be peaceful, living by the Ganga. That couldn't last, because when we did meet him we fell in love at first sight—my husband too, though he was not on the *bhakti marg.* Perhaps Chandra Swami *made* us love him, but that's another point.

Chandra Swami started to call me five times a day, to come to his ashram from where I was living, to do various jobs. He had me doing a lot of *seva,* and finally, after one year, I came to live in the ashram. Although my former guru was not happy about this he had in fact predicted it. More than a decade earlier in Canada he had forced me to learn to cook *chapatis.* Every night he called me to make *chapatis,* and I hated it and was angry about it. I said, "Why are you doing this? I hate it." He replied, "Because one day you will have an Indian guru and will be living in an ashram and be doing all the cooking." In fact, I spent five years in Chandra Swami's ashram kitchen cooking.

Everything that occurred previously just prepared me to live here. What happened with Chandra Swami was *seva*—I served the guru for ten years. If you serve the guru that means twenty-four hours on call. You have no personal life at all, and personal lives don't count. Some days you think you are going to die, and you still do it—that is *seva.*

I came to India to be happy and live with my spiritual

husband, to sit on the banks of the Ganga ten hours a day. But what happened was *guru seva*. This means you never expect to eat, sleep, be warm or live beyond today. You think that you will not live longer than today. One day, we all went to the mountains. I didn't have a shawl and friends had bought one for me. When we got there a beggar woman came over and Swamiji said, "Give the shawl to her." My friends protested and said, "Swamiji, Penny needs it!" He said, pointing to the beggar, "She needs it too." So I shivered through the day. Later we went shopping and, to my surprise, Swamiji saw some shawls and said, "Buy that one for Penny." (I should say that when I say Swamiji said something I mean he wrote it down or indicated it non-verbally because he is observing *mouna*, a vow of silence.) Anyway, later, at the hotel when we got back, he placed the beautiful shawl in my hands. For one moment I was so thrilled. Then, he took it out of my hands and gave it to the person next to me. In fact, some time later, he did give me another shawl.

Chandra Swami belongs to the Udasin lineage, which was founded by the youngest son of guru Nanak. So, in a way, guru Nanak is the supreme guru. Originally Chandra Swami did not emphasize his lineage, but he does more now. He teaches Vedanta, but perhaps he would disagree and say he just tells his experience. He has a definite way of teaching—he has been in *mouna* for many years, which is one of the most striking aspects. You ask a question, he writes an answer.

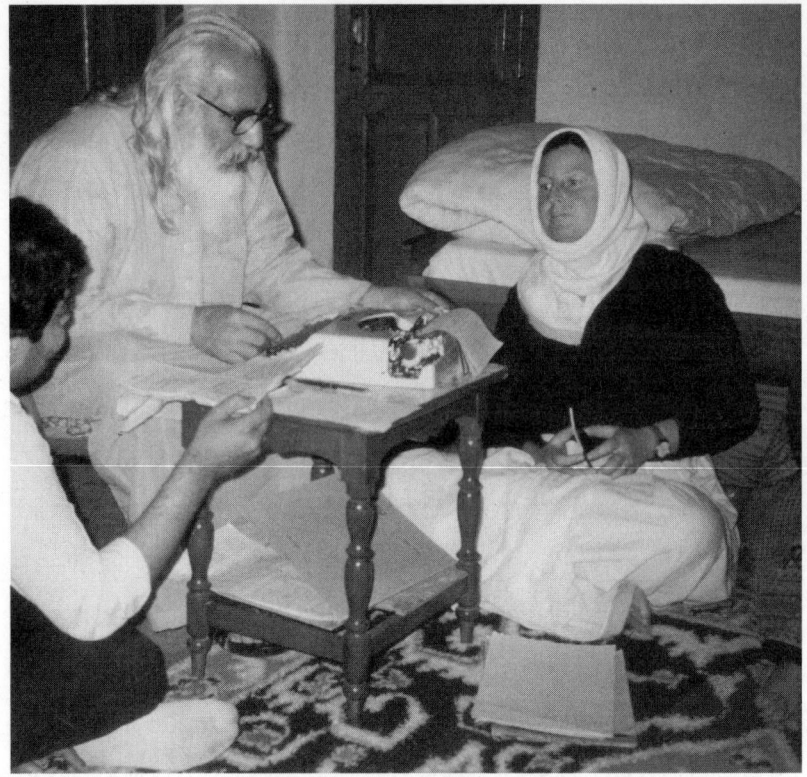

Penny Ma and Chandra Swami

I had a lot of years of ashram life, and one of the great things I experienced there was that in the ashram I'd be seen as a mother or as a policeman, and I had to accept both. At the ashram several Westerners went crazy, and they became my responsibility. One man chased me with an axe! These people were overwhelmed by the high level of energy there and could not handle it. One lady totally lost it—ripping off her clothes, tearing at people, violent and full of energy. We had to put her in a straightjacket. Chandra Swami said, "She'll be okay as soon as she gets back to her own country." I was slightly doubtful; even at the airport she was stealing people's food from their hands and lashing out. We arranged for a friend to meet her at her destination—it was out of the question for her parents to see her in such a state. Later, the friend who picked her up rang us and asked why we had bothered him, as she was totally normal. There were other examples of this happening. Swamiji was always right about these people. They returned to a state of relative normality when they left India.

Chandra Swami accepted my leaving the ashram thirteen years after I first arrived. My decision was not complicated or fly-by-night, I just felt called to a more solitary practice. Someday, somewhere, we have to sit alone and do *sadhana*. You can adore the guru without living in the ashram. He is still my guru, not only 'till "death do us part," but forever after. When I say that, what I mean is that he is my guru forever and ever, because the real guru is God.

The problem is that we should not ask the guru to be limited to the physical body—to be a guru of the body. We should want the guru to be the guru of the Spirit. If you just love the physical—supposing the guru gives in and lets you have him as the guru of the physical alone—then you will get the lesser of the two. What will happen is that you will go to the grave with a smile on your face, perhaps, but still be an ignorant fool.

There are many reasons why I remain in India after twenty years—there would have to be, as it's very hard for a foreign woman to live in India. I came because of the river Ganges. *Ganga Mayi* will do everything perfectly as she always has. There is a peculiar depth of overpowering strength and peacefulness on the banks of the Ganga, more so than in any other place in the world that I have traveled. The strength is *jnana,* spiritual wisdom or knowledge, that aids powerful meditation. The banks of the Ganga force you into peace. After three days here anyone can feel it (the Hindu scriptures have all the right terminology for this).

I broke a lot of people's hearts when I left my home. I brutally sacrificed a lot of things and continue to without heeding anyone's advice, so I should have a lot of good reasons to be here. I better! Age is a powerful force, I'm fifty-six, and in the last two years the element of age has entered my personality, and that is the most common reason to turn further to God. Thoughts you can't have when you are young, but at fifty-three-bingo, these thoughts will come in your mind. The

94

bottom line is I feel Ganga is taking care of me. I believe Ganga is literally my mother. I have no way to describe this but that is my experience. I feel such strong love, attraction and security. There is a magic in the water of the Ganga. I believe her to be the greatest physical manifestation of God.

Another main reason, and everyday confirmed, is the lesson to be learnt in the phenomena of order in chaos, which is embedded in Indian society as a whole. Total chaos. No stamps at the post-office, no water in the taps, no electricity, no one obeying any laws; no one obeying anything! That's just for starters. Everyone is overpowered by the experience on the roads— petrifying. The first time I experienced the roads from Delhi airport my mouth was open and I couldn't shut it. Every second I thought I was going to die. I still feel that when I drive now. But the chaos is outside since, in fact, the order is the inside of the people here—that's where everything works. They are extremely self-sufficient and alert, not brain-dead like in the West where everything is done for you. Here each individual figures out their own solution, whereas people in the West seem to have lost this resourcefulness. Indians are alert and alive, not just following a line.

The order is how everything works in spite of Indians! I love that because it has given me respect for my inner world. I cried everyday for about two years, initially, sad and frustrated by being screwed around and lied to so much. Now it's a privilege and a game. I know what to do and it has given me a stronger inner life.

Spiritual life in the West is a private little secret, like being in the closet if you are gay. But, in India your private life is expanding all the time and you have to have inward strength and your wits about you, because people are lying and cheating all the time and they're smarter than you, so you have got to get smart. In India, every time you turn around you are reminded about the spiritual life—saints are all over the place! In almost every home people are doing *puja*. From loudspeakers, from merchandise in shops, you are constantly reminded of religion. It is everywhere, and is alive and well. Every shop has a temple in it; can you imagine that in the West? You go to buy peanut butter and the shopkeeper goes to get it down and there is a picture of *Krishna* on the jar—isn't that wonderful! You see it all the time. I love to go shopping and find that the road is totally closed by a wedding, I love my plans to be overturned like that. Every morning when I wake up I hear *Ganga arati* from the loudspeakers here; everyday at Hari ki Pauri for two hundred years there are a thousand people doing *arati* to the Ganga. I think if you have the opportunity to come here and do *sadhana* you would be crazy to miss it.

My Western intellect is challenged here, or I am moved by what I see—perhaps by the sight of someone going into a temple with great reverence and bowing down. In the West churches are closing down, whereas in India there are tens of thousands of popular functioning temples, and new ones coming up. They are still being built in the old way where it takes twenty years to build. Inside the temples everything is always going on as it always has—people are cooking, meditating, singing, doing *puja*, having their heads shaved; or lying sound asleep, or getting dressed, or washing their clothes. All within the temple compound. I just sit in such places with tears in my eyes because this has gone on for thousands of years. The temples are alive and belong to the people; their faith is alive. In the West, if we ever had this it is now long gone; the poor priests have to advertise church picnics and still only a few will come. In places in India things may be very commercialized, but what is truly present is still there. The normal ceremonies of everyday life in India are still very meaningful.

India is a playful place, and when you are least prepared the Divine will make its presence felt. In the *murtis* the real Deity can make its presence felt at any moment. Statues can manifest the Real over and over again. This is the potential, and this is all over India! Powerful temple deities may go for a wander—there is such a temple in Vrindivan in which the deities have to be locked in a cage to prevent them leaving! There are so many *samadhis* of great saints, full of power. All sorts of things happen there, quite definitely. So much great spiritual history, so many great books written by real mystic scholars. What is important to the *sadhak,* the first rule, is good company—*sang (sangha)*. There is a good company everywhere here, all around; even if you live in Delhi.

Perhaps some of the ashrams are not what they once were. They have branched off. *Sannyasins* are straying as a group, getting highly involved in politics, becoming increasingly "worldly"—wanting cars and possessions. The pure *sannyasin* is dead against that. Times have changed, it is the Kali Yuga, and the next best thing we can hope for is that the spirit of *sannyas* becomes alive within.

It may not be the best road now for young people here to enter *sannyas,* as not a lot of meditation nor private contemplation goes on in many ashrams and they may get drawn into politics. An ashram should be a spiritual sanctuary, but they come to have their own *raison d'être,* their own needs. They want to expand and have an increasing income, and that influences the *sannyasins.* It is written very clearly in the Hindu scriptures that this is what will happen in the Kali Yuga—ashrams will become huge and fancy. They also say that households, few and far between, will become the spiritual centers.

I have come to believe literally in the Hindu scriptures and spend two hours a day reading from the *Srimad Bhagavatam,* the *Bhagavad Gita* or the *Vedas.* I think they are very reliable in the Kali yuga. They do not change. It is easy to study them in the East.

I have students, though I only teach minimal spiritual exercises. I am not a guru. I teach children *kirtan* and *japa;* I teach people to cope with the Kali yuga. I enjoy watching people be happy here. I feel I owe it to Ganga to create a haven, a place where people will be happy. The most I allow myself as far as shaping goes is to interest people in discovering the spiritual life—I sneak it in whenever I can, so you do feel that little bit of tension here.

I hope I will not be returning to the West. Since I've been in India for good I only went back once for four months. I wanted to see how things were. An Indian friend came with me, and sure enough my friend got fed up with the total and overwhelming lack of spirituality. The intensely spiritual atmosphere of India has spoiled me. The West was oppressing, and on an individual basis I found people extremely unhappy. Nor did I know what to do with people who did not believe in God, or themselves, or did not believe that they had an inner life. The first step they need to get to is: yes, there is a God, and yes, they have an inner life. But most people have not gotten there. Everyone is almost at that point when, in the night, they scream in terror at the misery of life. But they do a million things to avoid that moment—drugs, sex, marriage. Finally, you find out that the only thing to do is the ancient thing that brings peace of mind. We have the right to be happy. How much greater to go into the spiritual life happily rather than desperately. When I returned to India I kissed the tarmac! I'm happy here for God's sake.

*Sadhana* has to be transformed into an adventure. Then life becomes so exciting, you realize it is not you who is doing it— it is God. Each thing that happens to me, even if I turn on the TV,

I know God is doing it. I know that what I will see will be no accident This makes you lively and alert. Washing my hands is as important as anything else is; everything becomes *sadhana*. In my personal life chanting *Om* is as important as going to the bathroom. In the greater scheme of things, perhaps chanting *Om* is more important, but not individually, because I know that God is always directing my actions. Everything has a worth, and is of great value, because God has provided it; it is hurtful when people do not see the value of things, even their own lives. Each thing is to be cherished. God waits like a mother.

# 7

Rishikesh is known as the gateway to the Himalayas, historically a place of retreat and practice for *sadhus* and *sannyasins*. Although somewhat commercialized, Rishikesh retains much of its serene beauty and is a relaxing place to stay. The rocky beaches along the clear bubbling Ganges are particularly unspoiled and lovely. *Sadhus* and *sannyasins* still live in hermitages along the shore. In the thick jungle that surrounds parts of the town, Western students of yoga abound. They have their own cafes and hangouts around the Lakshman Jhula bridge—an area to be assiduously avoided at all costs, as far as I was concerned, unless one wanted to immerse oneself in an ambiance of aimless drifting, spiritual posturing, and of course, ganja smoking!

Many masters have made their homes in Rishikesh: Swami Sivananda, Tatwallah Baba, Swami Rama and Mastram Baba were all to be found here, until relatively recent times. Tatwallah Baba's tiny and practically inaccessible ashram is a beautiful reminder of the traditional living conditions of a forest dweller.

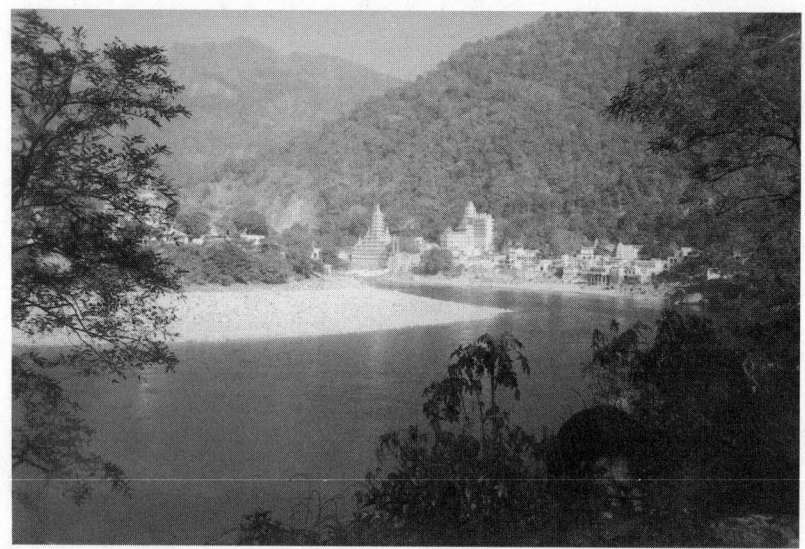

Rishikesh, beautiful and verdant. Although it looks like a picturesque resort, the multi-story buildings are all temples, not hotels.

Sadly, this saint was murdered by fanatics of one kind or another who also made an attempt on Swami Rama's life. Mastram Baba will be discussed in one of the following interviews; his cave on the beach is preserved and, again, the energy is pristine.

Swami Sivananda (1887-1963) was concerned with making the spiritual path available to as many people as he possibly could. He was a karma yogi "par excellence," writing hundreds of books and pamphlets on the various aspects of yoga philosophy. His works were designed to be accessible to the multitudes, but certainly there was no dilution of his message of loving God by serving and seeing Him in all. Sivananda set a good example of commitment to practice, though he encouraged others not to follow some of the more severe austerities he employed. In his earlier days he had stood every morning, for several hours, up to his neck in the freezing waters of the Ganga, repeating *mantras*—it spoilt his health in later years. He did not mind further wrecking his health with his relentless urge to serve others. On one occasion, during a particularly severe bout of sickness, his attendants did not stop by his room to assist him to the *bhajan* hall, knowing he badly needed to rest. It was with some horror, then, that they later found Swami Sivananda crawling along the ground on his way to *satsang!* The *kutir* where he lived is kept as it was during his lifetime—*bhajans* are held in this powerful shrine every evening.

Swami Sivananda was eclectic in his approach, and though belonging to the Saraswati order of Shankaracharya, whose lineage as we have seen is Saivite, his personal deity was Sri Krishna. After Swami Sivananda's *maha samadhi*, the running of his large ashram passed into the hands of Swami Chidananda, himself a student of Sivananda since 1943. Swami Chidananda is a respected teacher of Vedanta, and is the Guru to the next Western *sannyasin* interviewee, Swami Atmaswarupananda.

I met Swami Atmaswarupananda inside the Sivananda ashram just one morning after he had finished running a busy meditation retreat for Western visitors. His daughter joined us for the interview; she has also been initiated into *sannyas*. Swami Atmaswarupananda has a very straightforward, down-to-earth manner, which I appreciated. He is clearly serving his guru in whatever function that may require of him.

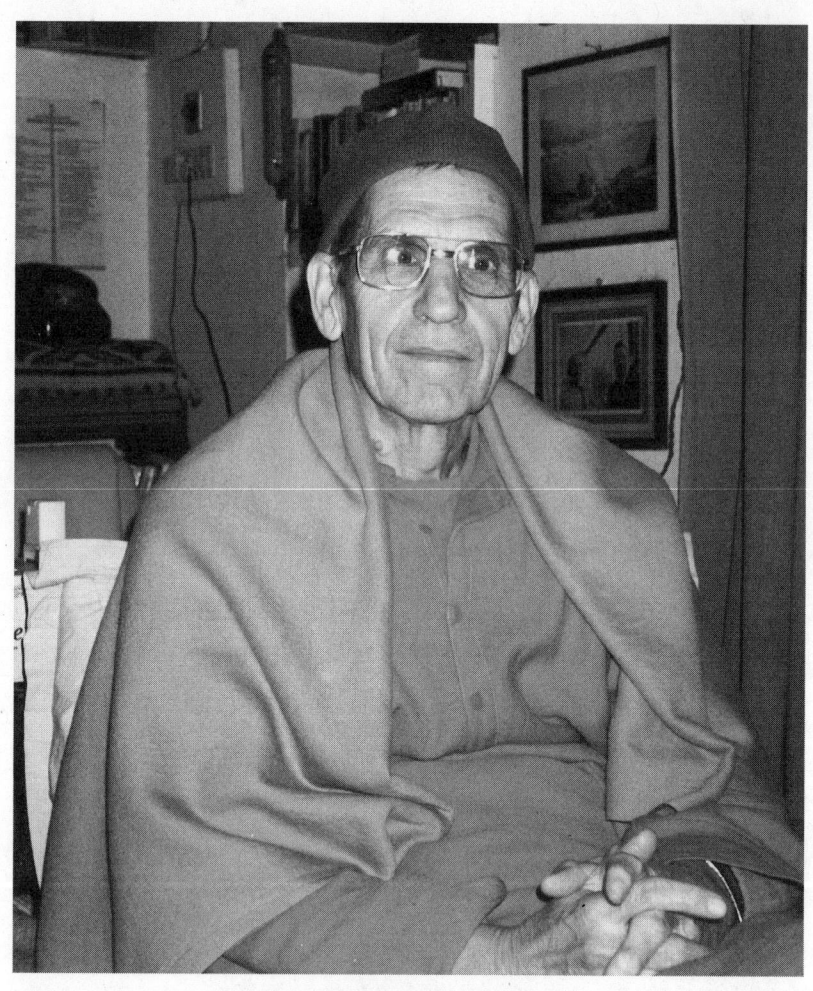

Swami Atmaswarupananda

# Swami Atmaswarupananda

When I first came to India I was hurting so much, due to leaving the family and the comforts of home, that it was almost a relief, or pleasure, to talk about my life. Now I find it difficult to do so; in fact, I find it to be a complete bore. But, anyway . . .

During the early fifties, when I was in my late twenties, I read two books, *In Tune With the Infinite* and *Cosmic Consciousness,* which had a profound effect upon me. I had been living a normal family life with fairly normal goals: I wanted to raise my family, make some money, and then perhaps go into politics and serve the country. These spiritual classics made me realize that there was a goal in life higher than the ones I had. I did a lot of further reading, but knew of no one in my own Protestant background who could take me further. So, my interest lay dormant for a number of years as I concentrated on business, community service, and raising my daughter and three sons.

One night, at a business meeting, a visiting Indian man sitting at my table casually referred to a state called *cosmic consciousness*. My interest immediately perked up, and I asked him if he had experienced it. He replied that he had—through the grace of his guru, Swami Sivananda. Our conversation continued and he gave me his card. Next day I called him, and over the following week or so had a number of conversations with him that simply thrilled me.

A year later, in 1960, I heard that one of Swami Sivananda's closest disciples, Swami Chidananda, was coming to Vancouver. I was completely taken by him. When he talked it was as if he was putting into words the thoughts that had been in my mind for years. I was so bowled over that if he had said, "Follow me," I probably would have done so, even though the children were still very young and I didn't have sufficient finances. Fortunately he didn't, but a guru-disciple relationship was formed that has lasted to this day.

I didn't see Swami Chidananda from 1961 until his next trip to the West in 1969. During that period he had succeeded Swami Sivananda as president of the Divine Life Society, while I had concentrated on business, marriage, and raising the children. Before he left in 1970, I casually asked him, "What next?" He replied, "Visit India some time." I asked, "How soon?" and he replied, "Within five years."

Somehow, that became a command for me. So, in 1973 I made arrangements with my partners to take six months off starting September 1974. Then, strangely, for seemingly completely different reasons, I resigned my position so that when I arrived in India in 1974 I had no firm commitments.

Before coming to India I had wondered whether I was perhaps meant to enter into an active spiritual life rather than return to business. As I was mulling it over one night an inner
voice said, "Leave it to Swami Chidananda." From that point on
the thought didn't arise again. Soon after arriving in India, I was
in a taxi with Swami Chidananda and he asked me about my
plans. I said that I was expecting to spend six months in India
and then meet my wife in Europe for three months before returning to Vancouver. Then, suddenly, I heard myself add, "But
how long I stay in India, or when and if I return to Canada, is up
to Swamiji." When I heard those words, I almost died—I realized
that I had just given my life away. However, the words were out,
and I had no desire to go back on them.

The long and the short of it is that he kept me here for
eighteen months and then sent me back to Canada for a four
month visit, which gave me an opportunity to straighten out my
affairs. He told me to return to India for an indefinite period.
Although I desperately didn't want to leave my family and the
comforts of home, I was determined to obey him, as I was convinced that his only concern was my highest good. It was very
difficult telling my family, but through some miracle, after getting over the initial shock, my wife became convinced it was
God's will and would then tell everyone, "If I can accept it so can
you." Thus, while it was very difficult to leave the family, through
God's grace there was no bitterness. And although I have only

seen my wife and three sons a couple of times since, our love has remained intact.

I returned to my old room in the ashram in August 1976 and have been here ever since. I haven't been back to Canada, but visited South Africa with Swami Chidananda in 1983; and last summer, my daughter (who has been here since 1980 and is now also a *sannyas*) and I spent a month in Hawaii, where we had a family reunion and I met my eight grandchildren for the first time.

About the only instruction Swami Chidananda ever gave me —except for giving me a routine to carry me over the first few months—was to sit quietly for a few minutes five or six times a day and to try and remember "who you are." In a nutshell, his teaching is "You are divine. Know this truth, and express it in your daily life." It seems to me that everything else is simply an elaboration of this basic theme.

My relationship with the guru is one of obedience, and I have now discovered that that is the root of my whole *sadhana*. Perhaps, if it is pure enough, it will lead to the death of the ego. The only purpose of the guru is to get rid of the disciple's ego, and if the disciple understands this and submits to it, then the relationship clicks.

I never asked for *sannyas*. Usually the disciple makes the request, and then the guru decides. As I was married, I had no thought of requesting it, but during the Christmas Eve celebrations in 1988, Swamiji surprised me by calling me over and

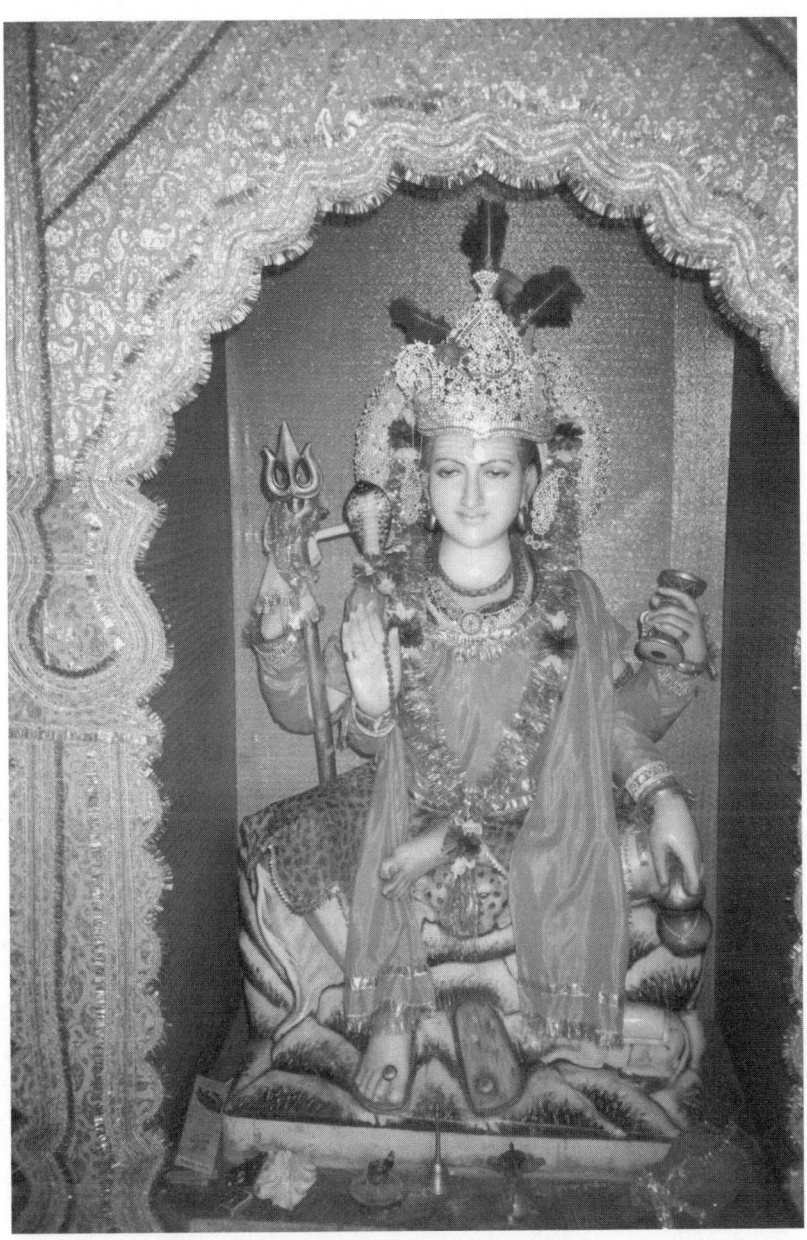

A fine white marble *murti* of Siva, in Rishikesh, is almost unrecognizable beneath the diamante and tinsel offerings.

giving me the cloth. The formal vows and my name came a couple of months later.

When I returned from Canada in 1976, I used to say, "The scriptures say that one of the most important things in the spiritual life is to have dispassion for the world. I am frank to admit that I don't have five cents' worth of dispassion. The world has treated me well." The strange thing is that now, after having lived over twenty years in India, where I find life difficult, I have developed a dispassion for my old way of life and its values. It is not that I reject the West, but I can now see the hollowness of my former values, and each year I become more and more convinced that the only answer to life is found in the words of Jesus: "Seek ye first the Kingdom of Heaven and all these things shall be yours as well."

I feel that there are many sincere spiritual seekers in the West. The greatest difficulty they seem to have is in sustaining their spiritual urge in a materialistic society. Their greatest complaint is one I had: it is so difficult to find anyone who wants to share your spiritual thoughts. Even the inspiration they receive after a visit to an ashram seems to dry up in that spiritual desert.

However, even such periods of spiritual loneliness can have a value. The spiritual life is no joke, and so unless you have known this deep loneliness, when the opportunity comes to enter the spiritual life, you may not be willing to pay the price. There has to be a hungering and thirsting after righteousness to carry you through the difficult periods.

As far as I can see, there are only two reasons I would now return to the West. The first is if my guru sent me, and the second would be if, for some unexpected reason, my visa was not renewed. The real significance of my shift to India, I believe, was that I was so identified with my old life that I needed to be pulled out of it right down to the roots. I sometimes joke that if I had been born a South Indian *brahmin*, I would have had to follow some Catholic priest to Alaska. But, of course, of equal importance is the privilege I have of living in a holy ashram founded by a great saint, in one of the most sacred parts of a basically spiritual country.

# 8

I first heard of Swami Jnanananda in Haridwar from a friendly French psychiatrist and student of Swami Vijayananda, Jacques Vigne. He had drawn a rough map of paths through the jungle leading to Swami Jnanananda's home. Equipped with this guide, I traveled further north and, unsurprisingly, soon became lost among the many seemingly identical tracks. I wandered through villages asking questions, sure that if a white *sannyasin* lived in the area the locals would know all about it! After several unsuccessful leads I paused at a shop stall and the owner pointed in the direction behind me and said, "Over there." I prepared myself for another long trek in a general but unspecified direction; however, the shopkeeper had spoken literally, for, as I turned round, there was Swami Jnanananda and a companion standing only a few meters away! He greeted me with warmth and interest, as though in fact he already knew me. His friend Maitri told me I was very lucky to find them there just at that moment, as Swami Jnanananda only came to this village once a week, for an hour or so, to buy a few provisions.

On travelling back to his home with him, I was relieved, quite sure that this remote spot would have taken several hours at least, and many more wrong turnings, to find.

Swami Jnanananda showed me around the hillside hermitage, much of which he had built himself. There is a peaceful, round hut for meditation, with mud walls and a thatched roof; this lovely environment has been constructed with practically no material resources—just a little skill and creativity. It saddened me to reflect on the squalid state of much of the housing and living conditions I'd seen both here in India and in the West. The insanity of ruthlessly destroying that which serves us most—nature—pressed in as I observed this ideal preservation of the traditional forest dweller's way of living. It is not a question of money, as television and consumer goods proliferate in the urban slums; more, a question of education and sensitivity to the powerful effect a pure and harmonious environment exercises on one's consciousness.

Swami Jnanananda cooked a delicious meal of *kedgeree* using herbs from the forest. It was a real pleasure to eat with one's fingers, to wash one's plate in the stream using a scourer of tough dried leaves and ash as a cleanser. A replenishing retreat from pre-packaged, plasticized modernity. I stopped to wonder why we had ever produced such a complex culture that so grotesquely manipulates all that is wholesome and natural, taking us further and further away from any sense of relationship to our environment. Afterwards, I took notes in Swami

Jnanananda's small *kutir*, which has a particularly striking feature: the ceiling is immaculately papered in gold foil, which reflects the light and makes the whole room softly glow. In the center of the ceiling is painted a large red *Shree Yantra*.

There is a great sense of lightness and joy present in Swami Jnanananda—a generosity of spirit. I could not help but notice the sprightly, enthusiastic energy and attention he brought to all of his actions, as though he had a great appetite and appreciation for even the mundane tasks of life. Walking with him that afternoon one had to have a brisk pace to keep up. I was a little amazed that this swami is in his sixties! Jacques Vigne has recorded an amusing anecdote about Swami Jnanananda in his excellent book, *The Indian Teaching Tradition*. After his departure for India, Swami Jnanananda's worried mother consulted C.G. Jung, the internationally reputed psychoanalyst in Zurich. Jung, who was at the height of his recognition, gave the following diagnosis: "It is a crisis of adolescence. Do not worry, he shall soon come back." Forty years later, it looks as though he may have been incorrect! Swami Jnanananda commented: "Jung, he was very young."

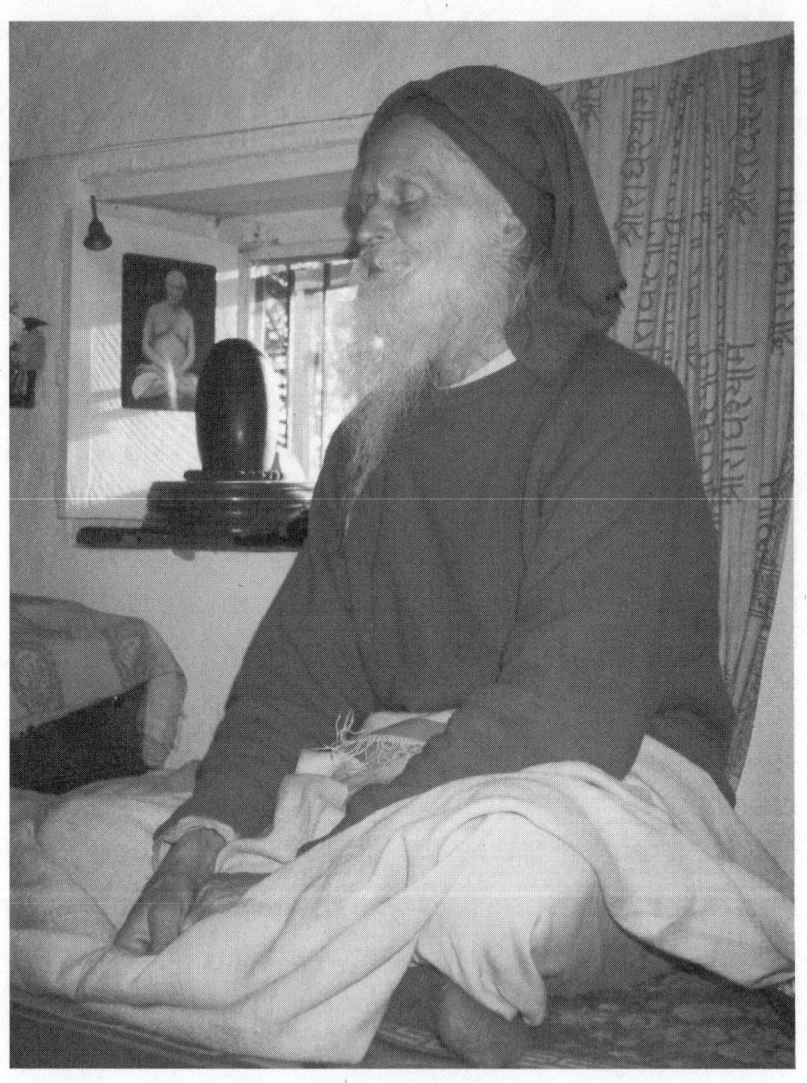

Swami Jnanananda

## Swami Jnanananda

I came to India in 1952 with just a small bag and two books, a pocket Bible, or the teachings of Christ, and Marcus Aureleus' meditations. From my early days I wanted to know the purpose of life; what one can attain within a lifetime. If I become an artist, what is the ultimate art? If I become a musician, what is the ultimate music? I tried all these things, very soon I realized there is no ultimate. I wanted to know the purpose of this life which is made up of so many moments. What is a moment of life, a moment of consciousness, a moment of existence? And, as I was asking these questions, I was asking "What is time?" The reply was, "We have no time to know what time is." Then my thoughts went to the East, for traditionally it has always been the place where people have found time to enquire into time.

You see, I didn't find any purpose in this life. What to do? Whatever one achieves, is there an ultimate satisfaction? Once I went to London to enroll at the Royal College of Music. They said, "You are too old." That's strange, I thought, hardly twenty and too old . . . already one life gone. It was only when I met the guru that I understood. He told me "You first look for God, then everything else will be given to you. We are all running after the lights and delights of the world, not realizing we are sacrificing God himself."

At twenty-three I came to India, leaving Switzerland and my past for good. I have never gone back. At the time of initiation the guru absolves you of your past, hence a new life—you enter the new life. It took me one week here to meet my guru, I had never heard of him before coming here. Coming to India in those days, at that age, wasn't so common. So many tried to discourage me, but as soon as I arrived here everything happened. The guru actually expected me, he knew I was coming on such and such a date. I did not know myself. He told a disciple that a person would arrive while he was away and to ask him—me—to wait three days. I waited. I could have chosen between two persons—each could have been my guru. But my natural inclination drew me to the person who kept me waiting. This was in Calcutta, Dakshineswar.

I stayed with him for twelve years—as long after I met him that he lived. After he left this world, I never returned to Calcutta; I stayed in the Himalayas. I waited three years before taking sannyas; first I lived as a brahmachari in the ashram.

My guru took me each year for five or six months to Rishikesh or Haridwar and gave me a place by the Ganges for meditation. During those twelve years I spent all my time by the banks of the Ganga. He taught *kriya* yoga. He insisted on regular practice. Along with renunciation, discipline is essential. There must be regular practice of a guru-given technique or *mantra*. In order to realize these practices I was drawn to complete renunciation—it is the best way to have sufficient time and to leave off thoughts of the world. The guru took care of me in every way. He blessed me for the future and he is still taking care of me now. His name was Swami Atmananda Giri. His guru was Swami Kevalanandan, Yogananda Paramahamsa's Sanskrit teacher. But my guru, Swami Atmananda Giri, actually took *sannyas* initiation from Yogananda. He was sixty-eight when he left the body; there was no need for another guru. He told me how to carry on; he told me before his passing.

I belong to the order known as Dasnaami *sannyasins,* which was founded in the ninth century by Adi Shankaracharya. *Sannyas* means renunciation, it is the fourth ashram or stage in Indian culture. The first is *brahmacharya*—student life.

The second is *grahastha*—the householder's life. The third is *vanprastha*—the life of retirement from worldly pursuits. The fourth is *sannyas*—the life of complete renunciation dedicated to the teaching of Divine knowledge.

The four divisions can be described like this: the first is one of addition, for a student must acquire knowledge; the second is one of subtraction, for a householder supports his family; the third is one of multiplicity, because having retired from the worldly life one has nothing else to do but acquire inner knowledge; the fourth is one of division—that is the time to distribute these inner riches for the enlightenment of others. So, really, to enter *sannyas* means to dwell in God.

I have been accepted by Hindus, legally also. There are some orthodox sections that may not accept this, but those in authority do. I became a *sannyasi* according to Hindu rites. This has been attested by the court, by the government. The guru said it would be of some use. According to a Hindu law, which is now not in vogue, by entering *sannyas* I automatically become a Hindu. But all spiritual teachings are the same: the essence is to dwell in God, to dwell in the Reality at all times. By spiritual practice one aims to lose one's little self, to become one with the Ideal.

I pass on what my guru taught me when there is a demand. There are some people who call themselves disciples. These teachings are in the traditional line, but specifically adapted to the individual. Beside the technical aspect of yoga, one has to pass on the subtler aspect, which leads to the ultimate transformation of each person who takes to the teachings. No two are alike. The exact nature of the teachings cannot be disclosed. It is beyond any words—call it grace, God's grace! To pass on grace and to be receptive to grace, that is itself grace.

My guru spoke to me in English, but there was not much talking; he asked me to practice what he taught me. Studying the ancient scriptures was my own liking; his emphasis was on regular meditation, discipline, and the remembrance of God. It was not a question of study from books to add to one's knowledge. It was surrender to the Divine, to feel what is meant by Reality or Absolute Truth. To feel this is to know it. Such feeling comes by intense self-giving. It is the grace of the unspeakable power of the Divine that opens the way to bestow the new life.

What causes us to be drawn to a particular guru? Everything is due to past determination. There must be sincere longing, sincere prayer, plus God's grace. It is that grace and the blessing of some good soul. Such good souls are everywhere in the world. The blessings of a good soul in the West may help a person to go to the East. If people wish to break away from ignorance and they haven't yet found a guru, they should pray to God ceaselessly for a guide.

After finding a guide, a teacher, they should serve him in any way they are capable, and follow the teachings as far as possible. If one does not have a guru one should at least cultivate the company of good persons, seekers of the way. One can learn much from them. I would say it is essential to have a living teacher. However, if one is false, the guru will also be false. In the guru-disciple relationship there are many obstacles, the greatest being doubt. There will be persons questioning the disciple: "How do you know if your guru is realized; if he is competent?" They may try to awaken doubts—and should there be doubts, this is not a true disciple. Personally speaking, I found that the guru who happened to be guru to me was much better, more evolved than I was, so it was to my advantage to follow him. One follows the guru because one wants to follow God, and if one is sincere in following God, then the guru will become the instrument of God.

Also, it is not a question of my guru and your guru and someone else's guru—there is only *The Guru*. "Guru" is a state of consciousness—it's not a person. The person is only the instrument through which the power of the guru flows. Hence to say "my guru" is belittling the guru. It's also the cause of much confusion. To have a guru usually means one gets initiation from him, but some gurus don't give formal initiation. It depends entirely on the guru's will.

Meditation depends on the guru's instructions, which are usually given in secret. But essentially, meditation means to quiet the mind. More than that, to quiet oneself. That means to be silent in mind, body, feelings, thoughts, above all to be steady at heart within, for at heart *"Thou art."* To be steady in the innermost center of one's being or consciousness, the practice of equanimity, practice of renunciation, practice of the remembrance of God, are essential. Then alone one can take refuge in the innermost silence itself. It's inexpressible.

The particular time to meditate is one of the conditions laid down by the guru. It should go on indefinitely, irrespective of any thought that one has realized or not realized anything. But, of course, the whole day should be spent in practicing the presence of God, practicing the presence of that Being. I sit in the early morning—it's called the hour of Brahma—four o'clock 'till sunrise. This is traditionally the time when the yogis and *sannyasis* practice meditation. The difference between a beginner and an adept is that, for the beginner it's an effort, for the adept it's natural. Every sort of practice becomes natural in the course of time. But here we are dealing with the intrinsic nature of one's own self being. So, one can say that when meditation becomes one's own nature, it is natural.

I don't observe any rituals of my own; sometimes I observe those of my friends. To place a flower in a vase is a ritual. One can make one's whole life a ritual without making it a rite. Everything can be a ritual if all one's actions are offered to God. A ritual means to commune with God.

The sort of uniform a *sannyasin* wears is helpful in the beginning; it's like hedging a small plant, because like this, one is not troubled by the world. One ultimately outgrows the color. One ultimately outgrows all outward signs. In the life of renunciation, simplicity is foremost.

In the path I follow, marriage is not advocated. It is a way taken after one has done with the world. But, generally speaking, marriage is no obstacle to the spiritual path. Most *rishis* and sages of bygone times were married. The path of renunciation of sensual desire is not advisable for young people: it is advocated in exceptional cases, when the guru, through insight, knows it is possible. Generally, one should pass through the life of a householder, but on reaching a certain stage, retire from the worldly life—it can be done along with one's wife—and then devote one's time entirely to the spiritual life. It is the natural evolution of man that he should retire from material involvement when he grows old, wherever he lives. Otherwise, the purpose of life is unfulfilled. Family life, earning money for reasonable living, doing good for one's country, *et cetera*, is called *dharma*—good actions. This one should do. But, above all, one should know how to retire from these outer actions, because the inner life also has a demand. The later stage of one's life is for contemplation—everything becomes subordinate to realizing God.

As regards the hectic conditions under which most people live in the West, I believe the time will come when only those who meditate will be able to sleep at night. The total dependence on money and the security we imagine it brings is total ignorance if we are afraid to be alone, without material possessions. At the time of death, even millionaires are alone—nothing outside can help us. We are alone with our fears if we are rooted in the body, and we carry those impressions with us into the Beyond. Those who have meditated will also be alone when they leave, but will be filled with peace, and they will carry that peace with them. Life can be beautifully enriched by inner silence, what you may call silently loving, silently feeling, silently thinking. Such a life fulfils the purpose of life. That is to live correctly. If we live correctly we are able to face death fearlessly. That incident in life known as "death" we have to face without fear, otherwise death becomes distorted and we cannot pass through it in peace. So, if we find the right way of living, the secret way of dying will be revealed. Death is the door through which we pass into life renewed.

In truth, there is neither East nor West—there is one humanity. These teachings are eternal; they propagate the eternal; they help humanity to realize that which is eternal. Man's involvement in materialism is an experiment; he plays with nature and nature plays with him. Gradually man wants to become the master, so he puts away his toys and looks towards himself to find a marvel—there is no greater creation than himself. He can then probe the mystery of his own being, and it is here that the eternal teachings come as a guide.

So, anybody, anywhere, can follow such teachings. For someone like myself, India seems to be the place for this life's evolution, but that does not mean that those who yearn for the new life cannot find it in the West. We should go beyond the names and forms they represent and arrive at the nameless, the formless Truth that has its being everywhere. It is universal understanding, universal realization, complete identification with the higher life that alone brings salvation to Christians in the West, as well as to Hindus in the East.

If you are in a quest of the truth, you cannot get the untruth. Life changes for everyone; while living in this life we are to start the new life. The new life has to become the real life, then only is it to be mentioned as something auspicious. Otherwise the new life may change into a newer life, or even change back into the old life. The question is, Who is living? What is life? What is the aim of life?

Although I live a solitary life, there is no such thing as loneliness. One likes company for the sake of spiritual discussion, for the sake of *satsang,* for the give-and-take which is part of life. The reason why there is no such thing as loneliness is because when one is alone, one is alone with God, and when one is in company, one is in company with God.

The owner of the estate where I now live met me when I was living on the banks of the Ganga. He suggested I should try the solitude of the forest. Reluctantly I came here. At first I stayed only a few months at a time; it has now become a kind of permanent abode. When I am here I manage everything myself, but a *sannyasi* is homeless—it is one of the conditions. The whole world is his home, and as such he is not bound by any one place. Living the simple way has never been a problem because everything had to be given up; everything had to be forgotten.

We should never forget—those of us who have been drawn to live in India—we are living here by God's will. The spiritual life is the beginning, the middle and the end of all life; everything is subordinate to the spiritual idea; everything else is a play. I found that the one great difference between the East and the West is that, in the West, everything of this world seems real, whereas, in the East, one sees everything is a play, and only God is real.

# 9

Somewhat reluctantly I left the fine company of Swami Jnanananda for an eight-hour bus ride further north—deep into the Himalayan foothills. It's difficult to relax for the first hour of this journey: roads are narrow, with sheer drops of hundreds of feet to one side. The well-used (everything in India is "well-used") buses careen along at a fair speed, and one is often very close to the edge of the precipice! Knuckles turn white, teeth grind, fear runs up and down one's spine: death, in a rather terrifying manner, is an imminent possibility. However, observing the calmness of one's fellow Indian passengers restores a sense of balance. Perhaps it is not such an ordeal, though the bumper stickers—with grinning demons' heads and "Uphill all the way!" emblazoned across them—on the passing trucks and buses, is disconcerting. It feels as though this pithy statement may be the local ethos, as the mountain people have a guarded, even somewhat gruff, manner. A little experience reveals this to be just a show. They are guileless and soft, and pride dictates a tough front.

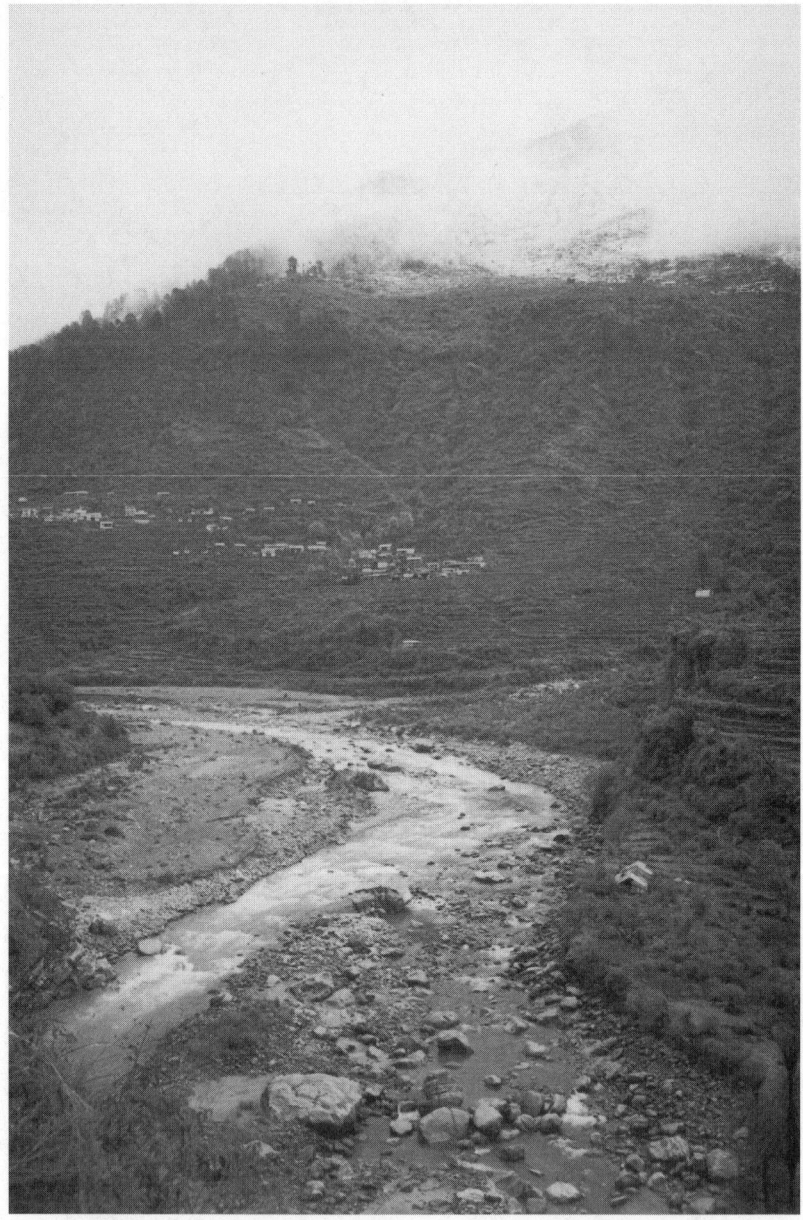

The Ganges at the foothills of the mighty Himalayas, not far from the secluded hermitage of Nani Ma.

The views are breathtaking: majestic panoramas of green valleys, distant plains and grand snow-peaked mountains. The Ganges coils its way around the bases of the hills, like a fabulous creature of myth—a gleaming, cerulean blue snake.

A day later I found Nani Ma's home with the help of two village boys who escorted me for an hour through gray drizzling rain, excited at the prospect of a postcard from London on my return. A few attractive wooden huts, right beside the rocky banks of the foaming Ganga, house a handful of devotees of Sri Mastram Baba. Nani Ma suggested we talk in the hut, which serves as a shrine to her now deceased guru.

Ascending the steps of the hut I faced a wall of photographs of a handsome *sadhu* with an impressive penetrating gaze and a radiant golden complexion. The hermitage is pared down and simple, similarly I found Nani Ma to be quiet and self-effacing— though not without passion.

The genuine ordinariness I met in Nani Ma took me by surprise as I had heard many stories about the exactingly austere *sadhanas* she has practiced. I suppose what enabled her to perform such acts of *tapas* successfully was this same ordinary, even humble, approach.

# Nani Ma

I was twenty-two when I arrived in India on the hippie trail in 1971; of course a lot of people were coming to India then. Before I had come I'd spent six months in Morocco and had heard a little about India. Like many people I was fairly fed up with the West and society at that time, and was looking for something more uplifting. I came overland. I arrived with very little money—thirteen rupees, not very much! Taking a train to Delhi I was then penniless, and stayed in the garden of a little hotel where some friends were staying. After some adventures I went with a South American and a Finnish gentleman to Almora in their jeep. There I saw a procession of people doing *kirtan*, including a foreigner who I asked what was happening. He told me they were doing devotional singing to their guru. That was the first time I had heard the word *guru,* so I asked where such people lived, and he informed me "on the banks of the Ganga."

Time passed and I was resting at Ram Nagar because of injured feet. Here I met a pundit who was a devotee of Sri

Mastram Babaji who indeed lived on the banks of the Ganges, in Rishikesh. A few days later he took me to him. By this time I had read the *Bhagavad Gita*, and in the second chapter a realized sage is described. Since then I had been praying, non-stop, that I would meet a realized guru and none other. So I kind of felt my prayers would be answered because they were so desperate! When I walked into his "ashram" (he lived in a cave), I already knew I was home. There was no doubt, even before I saw him, that this was "it." It was monsoon time and he was living under a tarpaulin. It was dark and there was such an incredible peace—I'd never felt such vibrations in my life. I hardly spoke to him at first; I just watched the beauty of the place. It stilled the mind. There did not need to be any speaking, it was already an accepted fact—I knew I was not going anywhere for the rest of my life.

We had a short talk in which he explained how impossible it would be for me to live there. We spoke through a translator. I was given a little place to sleep on a veranda nearby, where some of his household devotees stayed. I was straightaway totally entranced, in love in a Divine way—absolutely sold forever; and it's still the same twenty-seven years later. Mastram Baba was the only one for me who never disappointed, ever. There has been no reason to leave him, even though he's not physically present. He left his body in 1987.

It was in 1971 that I first met him, so I was with him for sixteen years. The ashram was just a cave on the beach and its surrounding area. The male *sadhus* lived in the other caves, and the ladies had to stay outside, and came to the "ashram" from three a.m. to ten a.m. Not for his benefit, for the other *sadhus*.

I didn't really have any practice. Traditionally you start off with a large portion of *seva* (service), some study, some time with the guru, and some meditation. These proportions change as the student advances, until it should be mainly meditation, until Realization. The first few years I mainly swept the ashram paths (i.e., the rocks and sand), and picked up cow dung to make pats for fuel, freshly plastering his cave and platform, and taught the poor children who gathered there. I also performed a *puja* to Siva everyday, offering flowers and water, and bathed in the Ganga everyday, too.

There were a lot of cows about; he used to feed them. He didn't touch money so his disciples bought the food. If anyone asked him what to do, he wouldn't readily say anything, but he allowed his devotees to feed anyone that came, and to feed the cows. We would eat what was left over—or what was not left over, as the case may be. That was in the early years; later on, food was cooked in a nearby house. Two or three hundred would come to eat during the summer, up to fifty in the winter, and on festival days perhaps a thousand. His household disciples would give his *sadhu* disciples clothes, but he had only one cloth, and that was all you could give him. Nor would he allow any structure to be built except out of straw or rough wood.

My *seva* gradually became less. I learned Hindi and Sanskrit, enabling me to study Vedanta, the *Puranas,* and other classical texts. When the study lessened, meditation increased. You know, after arriving I never actually left. Once, after thirteen years, I had to run around for a visa. In-between, he sent me with someone to see some holy place, and I showed him, in the *Mahabharata,* a passage where it states that the guru's feet is the holiest of places. After that he never sent me anywhere else—I never wanted to go to any other place. I did quite a lot of fasting and *tapasya* in those days. He didn't tell me to do this, but if I asked him he would say yes.

Babaji did not easily give instruction, but, if asked, he would give direction. I'd say, "The *rishis* did this or that, should I?" His only real instruction, when I was ready for it, was meditation. His *satsang* was the most important thing, which was why I learned Hindi so quickly, so I could understand him. Any teaching was usually questions and answers, completely informal: Him sitting on a rock or on the sand, walking or lying down. Babaji did not speak much, but whatever he said had tremendous depth and was easy to understand. Every word that came out of his mouth was something you could use for the rest of your life. He was very inspiring and encouraging. After seven or eight years he told me my path from past lives was meditation, and apart from the last year, when his body was fairly ill, I spent all my time in mediation. This is more or less all I've been doing for the last ten years, with some study also.

Mastram Baba never said anything about his background. We never knew where he was from, his age, name or village . . . nothing. Still, he often told us stories about his wanderings and childhood, from which we know he was a Brahmin and that he left home in his mid-teens after a traditional Sanskrit education. In the middle years, before he became known in Rishikesh, Haridwar and Badrinarian, he had wandered on foot all over India. His wandering was as the *rishis* did—barefoot, with one cloth, and no possessions; living under trees or in temples; not spending more than one night in any place. He lived on what we call *arkash vritti*, which is living on whatever you get, totally un-asked-for, including not going to places where food is given out. Nor did he ever take anything from a cultivated field or carry a water pot. He was an extreme example of renunciation. Some-where during that time we can only assume that he gained the knowledge he had when he became known as a *jnani*.

He said he had both an outer and an inner guru, but never anything about living with or following them. Once he remarked that a true *adikari* (advanced seeker) had to hear a *mahavakya* only once to become a realized guru. As far as we know, that was what his circumstance was.

Once he left the body I missed him for a while, a great deal, being unable to ask him spiritual questions. But I was confident in his teaching always, and now I realize that he is not confined to his body. That is not the only way he can teach. Now I find him teaching through the scriptures, and through everyone, every-

135

where. There is a point in *sadhana* when everything becomes the guru; *everything* is him, so there is no room to miss him. I have complete confidence that he is going to take me where I want to go—so that's his problem! I just believe and have complete faith in him. He once told me that the disciple is like a sheep that is caught in barbed wire, and the guru is the farmer who is trying to pick him out. If the sheep keeps still, the job is much easier; otherwise he keeps getting caught up again and again. As one's faith increases, one sees this; then there is not really any problem. Not *much* anyway.

What was special about Sri Mastram Babaji was that he *was* what he taught—you didn't only have his words, you had his example, which is what made his words so powerful. He had absolutely no interest in anything worldly; he did not need anything. He was completely self-sufficient in every way, and was so full of happiness, so full of bliss, that you knew, just by looking at him, that there was something much better to be had than anything you had seen or known.

For me, since he's gone, it's been a teaching that the realized guru is never gone.

He's always there. Babaji said: "A realized guru is like a wish-yielding tree. He wants to give everything and he has everything to give. People bring such little pots."

Many things in my former life primed me for the relationship—more or less everything. I'll just say I already was very dispassionate, and had no faith in anything I'd seen in the West.

Babaji said that if one really wants the true guru, then the true guru knows, because he is the Self. Then he will call you to him. Otherwise you can't find him by looking for him, because he is beyond the mind and intellect. Even if you see a realized guru you can't recognize him unless he wishes you to. In this case, either I was ready or he was ready to give his grace, so he allowed me to find him. There was nothing extraordinary about me staying with him, because if you saw someone full of infinite love and infinite knowledge, why would you leave him?

I still pray that my intellect never becomes clouded so that I would leave him, but Babaji also said: "The true guru is like a tiger. Once he captures his prey he doesn't get away. If the guru wants you, you won't be able to get away, even if you want to." That's just his grace, otherwise we are so stupid, what could we do without grace? That God wanted to take over your life completely—that is supposed to be the be-all-and-end-all of life. There is nothing complicated about the spiritual path; we are complicated. The guru is simple, and the truth is the disciple should be too, but those things are not always together. All I wanted to know was the way out, liberation; and the guru is the door.

Now I am an Indian citizen. I love everything about India, and the things I don't love I understand. I never felt really at home in the West. I would *now* (there is no difference anywhere now), but then I didn't feel that. No one can say what will happen in the future, but there is nothing there I would go back for, having been in India for nearly half my life.

The Westerners I have met have great intellectual knowledge and understanding but their actual behavior on a spiritual
level is usually very far behind. You can have a discussion on
Vedanta, but in India people have more understanding about
love and the fact that God is everywhere. When it comes down
to it, Westerners are very much isolated units. That's been my
impression. They're not open. But in India, if they learn anything
they learn to become open, and if they can get over their fear,
they have a chance of learning something. They don't know how
to function as a whole. This India teaches: that we are part of a
greater body, not something by ourselves. Many Westerners
that come *do* want to stay, as they experience love for the first
time. They receive it and they see it. Then, of course, if they are
exposed to the authentic scriptures, there is a whole new world.

I teach as little as possible, not really "teaching." People
come, they ask questions and I answer. If it's helpful to them
then I suppose it's a teaching. I certainly don't want to teach, I'd
rather learn something first. If you've met someone like Babaji
then you are not quite so quick to teach, because you don't
forget what you are when you have a proper example like that.
Teaching can be helpful in that you learn yourself as you teach,
but it possibly wastes good *sadhana* time.

My guru said that reaching for liberation is like climbing a
high, steep mountain. If you put out your hand to help someone
before you've got to the top you might just lose your balance

and fall off. But if you keep climbing up to the top, then, when you are sitting firmly at the peak, you can tell everybody the way and how to come. So I'm wary of teaching, even if it may seem helpful to some.

# 10

Entering the area of Vrindivan is akin to waking up in a colorful dreamland where all the usual rules and regulations fall away, to an extent. All that matters here is the love of the god Krishna, as supremely embodied in his lover and beloved devotee Sri Radha, and in her milkmaid friends, the *gopis*. A mood of joy and innocence permeates the town—a sense of joyous play appropriate to the land in which Krishna spent his carefree youth as a cowherd, some five thousand years ago. Wherever you wander in Vrindivan the local people and fellow pilgrims greet you with a friendly "*Radhai, Radhai,*" and sometimes with a beautiful gesture in which they raise the index finger of the right hand, point it upright and swirl it in a circular, clockwise direction. Symbolically this means, "You are coming closer to the Divine," and is a wonderful invitation to mutual remembrance of God.

The depth of the people's devotion to Krishna is reflected in the unprecedented number of temples, both ancient and modern, dedicated to His worship—there are at least four thousand.

Extravagant displays of florid architecture abound, and create a dizzying eclectic townscape. Much of the town is in a state of decay, which somehow adds to the appeal.

The most popular temple in Vrindivan is that of Banke Bihari, a name that refers to Krishna in the form of the Supreme Enjoyer. The deity was found in a well by Swami Haridasa, some-time in the fifteenth or sixteenth century, and the present temple was constructed in 1864. Tatiasthan, the headquarters of the Haridasa sect, so impressed the great Indian saint, Neem Keroli Baba, that he said that one had not visited Vrindivan unless one had visited Tatiasthan. I was told that the *mahant* of the sect had not left this compound for fifty years.

Tatiasthan is extraordinary. One steps through a small gate in a wall to find oneself in an ancient jungle of twisting trees and hanging creepers. The ground is covered with the softest white sand that once covered all the land of Vrindivan. A special tree has the name of Radha formed in hundreds of places all over its bark, and I could see branches where the name was in the process of formation—naturally. It was not carved on.

Banke Bihari temple is approached through a series of busy narrow lanes packed with stalls that sell every kind of article imaginable for the worship of deities. There are oil lamps of all sizes, small ornate thrones and swings on which the deity's im-age can be placed, incense, peacock feather fans for fanning the deity, toys to be given as gifts to the deity, and an endless variety of miniature garments in jewel-bright shades in which to

142

dress the deities. Outside the temple a long row of flower sellers do a brisk trade, their luscious fresh garlands impregnate the air with the heady perfumes of rose and jasmine. Inside, a delicate canopy of tangerine-colored marigolds adorns the ceiling, and the shrine itself is festooned by a great crescent of rainbow-colored gladioli. The atmosphere is lush and ripe—full of anticipation and desire for Krishna's *darshan*. It was in this place that Sri Ramakrishna went into *samadhi* at the sight of the idol.

As I stand there taking in all the sights and smells, a *pujari* whips open the plush velvet curtain covering the shrine, only to pull it closed four seconds later. A great sigh ripples through the crowd at the brief sight of Banke Bihari. After a few minutes full of plaintive longing, the curtain opens again, and once more the crowd express their appreciation with sighs of satisfaction.

The *pujari* plays with these love struck devotees giving them just the tiniest peek of their beloved Krishna, teasing them, making them wait until, in a dramatic and magnanimous gesture, he throws the curtain open revealing the splendid *murti* for long minutes.

Banke Bihari is bewitchingly beautiful, his face dazzling jet-black with enormous scarlet-rimmed eyes that stare out in an intoxicating reverie—the Lord looks mad! His smiling lips are pursed above a golden flute, the sweet music of which is said to irresistibly lure one into his enchanting realm. Certainly it seemed that many there the night I visited were listening to that melody. I felt transfixed to the spot at this image of God, so bizarre to Western religious and aesthetic sensibilities; in fact I was a little shocked! Banke Bihari felt full of mystic power, and the joyous dark form communicated directly to the heart something about the nature of the Divine that is practically unheard of in the West—a love without reason, a creation solely for the play of the Lord. A delightful revelation hit me—God is unhinged! A playful crazy lunatic with a love so absolute it transcends all reason. Then, like the devotees around me, I was left simply gasping in appreciation as the curtain closed once more. As though to treat a fever, a *pujari* came by and graciously covered the faces of devotees with cooling sandalwood paste.

The story behind Lala Babu, another of Vrindivan's glorious temples, is delightfully inspiring. Lovely as a jewel, with its soaring golden sandstone towers, the temple was founded by a rich businessman, Krishna Chandra Sinh. At the start of the eighteenth century he decided he wanted to put his wealth to some worthwhile use, and accordingly had this temple constructed. Its completion exhausted all of his resources, and he spent the rest of his life living as a simple *sadhu* begging on the entrance steps. He became known as Lala Babu.

Vrindivan's dusty lanes teem with life, and due to Krishna having been a cowherd, cows are especially well represented. These fine beasts are everywhere, and perfectly at ease slowly cruising through town, scavenging as they go. These animals are different from their Western counterparts—Indian cows are confident! Locals feed them, pet them, worship them, and the cows for their part bestow gentle and loving glances in return. Actually, the sanctity in which the cow is held in the Vaishnavite fold has reached a height that, to the uninitiated foreigner, seems positively surreal. Cow *seva*—the service of cows—is considered one of the best *sadhanas* a *sadhu* can practice. I encountered a friendly group of *sadhus* who were doing just that, with a herd of a hundred cows to care for.

It is important to realize that these *sadhus* have no money and have to beg to procure food for both themselves and their cows, which are looked after in an exemplary fashion. No financial "exploitation" is involved here—the animals are not kept for dairy farming purposes, and their milk is not sold. They are kept because they are considered dear to God, and deserving of respectful protection and service for their own sakes. Perhaps only in India could one spend one's life worshipping cows as one's chosen spiritual path.

The other much loved and much loathed inhabitants of Vrindivan are the *bhandas*—monkeys. The town has swarms of them; their chattering community living on the rooftops. Before arriving I had heard the story that some years ago a snack-seller had trained a single *bhanda* to snatch eyeglasses from people's faces. The animal would only return the glasses when given something to eat from the snack-vendor's stall. It was a rather cute trick, and the vendor's sales duly increased. Now, however, this situation has escalated out of all proportion, as all the monkeys soon learned this new and easy method of obtaining food. The monkeys also found that they could extract more food by not actually returning the spectacles at all! Masses of heartbroken pilgrims found their visit to holy Vrindivan ruined by being deprived of their sight. Not only that, the monkeys became ever more wild and daring, and were up for stealing anything they could—keys, hats, cameras, purses and handbags. The "game" got so bad that the government had to act, and thousands of monkeys were captured by trained handlers and taken to a reserve specially set up for that purpose. The story made for great PR, and was televised throughout India.

Unfortunately, this government intervention happened some time ago, and it is still in the food vendors' interests to ensure that the remaining monkeys, of which there are many, are well rewarded for similar stunts. An Indian gentleman I met and with whom I was somewhat reluctantly touring the town, took no notice of the much-publicized warnings, and so I had the unexpected pleasure of observing the *bhandas* in action. As the gentleman and I walked down a lane together, a monkey ran up behind him at great speed, and with some dexterity leaped onto his shoulder. In seconds, the *bhanda* had snatched the man's specs away and was gone. Help soon arrived in the form of a street urchin armed with a stick and a *chapati*—it was all quite amazing. A humorous scenario unfolded with the irate gentleman ferociously arguing with a food vendor over the price of this single *chapati* indispensable for the safe return of his glasses. This gentleman had sponged money off me all day for food, newspapers, and rickshaws, and was now complaining vociferously and indignantly about the conniving tactics of this band of devils acting as shopkeepers! Nonetheless, it was myself who had to furnish him with the few rupees needed to bring this entertaining drama, which most of the street now seemed to be involved in, to a close. He later disclosed to me that these people would take every penny a person had!

There is a secret garden in Vrindivan known as Seva Kunj, outside of which ladies sell small bags of puffed rice. I wondered what exactly the rice was for until one of them, by way of demonstration, hurled a handful into the air. Instantly we were

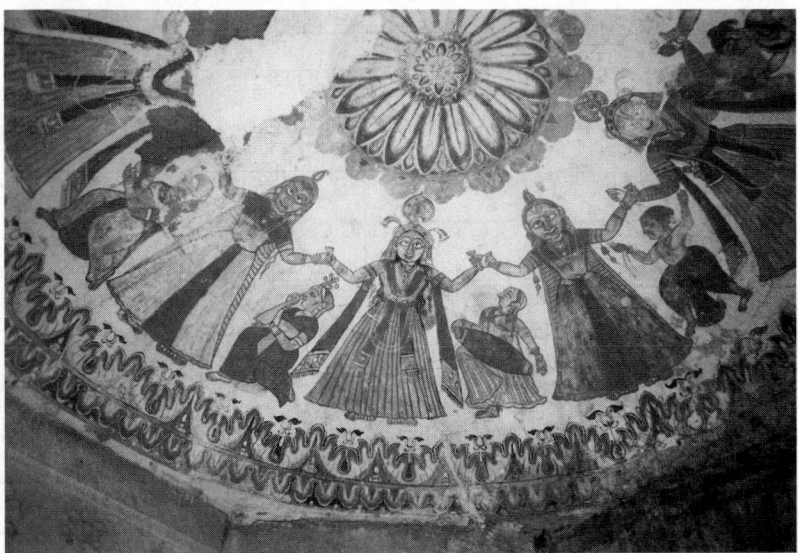

The Ras Lila painted on an unprotected and now crumbling ceiling of the Krishna Sarovar temple, near Vrindivan.

surrounded by a dozen snarling monkeys fighting with one another over the scattered grains. Seva Kunj is a mysterious grove where every evening Krishna is believed to perform the *Ras Lila* with Radha and the *gopis*. The platform where this Divine love play is said to occur has been "helpfully" covered in concrete by the town municipality. Yet, despite the ugliness of the concrete and the mounds of monkey-droppings that one inevitably treads on (bare feet only are allowed)—the garden retains a special atmosphere. It is well known among the local people, known as *braj bhasis*, that anyone staying overnight in Seva Kunj will face dire consequences—usually death.

Penny Ma told a remarkable story to this effect. A lady she knew had been given the task of accompanying an Indian devotee of her guru to Vrindivan so he could have pundits perform the rituals appropriate for the coming of his sixtieth birthday. The gentleman was determined to stay overnight in Seva Kunj to see for himself what went on there after dark. The lady felt very uncomfortable about this, and extracted a promise from him that he would do no such thing. Needless to say, he slipped away and did just that, hiding in the bushes when the gardens—keepers did their evening rounds, checking that no one was left in the garden before they locked it. The old man had concealed himself in a spot where he could observe the platform in secrecy, and as night fell, to his astonishment something *did* occur. Two celestial *gopis* appeared and started to sweep the platform, preparing it for the *Ras Lila*. As they gracefully worked one of them spotted the gentleman and became very angry—she paced over to his lair and struck him hard across the head with her broom. Gripped with an agonizing pain he spent the rest of the night in the garden in a state of paralysis, unable to see. When he was found the next morning barely hanging onto life, he was rushed to hospital. The lady who had accompanied him had become aware that he was missing and had gone to the garden, where her worst fears were confirmed. At the hospital she found him barely conscious and still in intense pain. He managed to scrawl down what he had seen on a piece of paper. Then, he died. Penny Ma met the lady shortly after this incident, when she was still in a state of shock over this turn of events.

Near to Seva Kunj is another garden, Nidhuvana, where Radha and Krishna are said to retire after performing the *Ras Lila*. A small temple contains a bed for the Divinities' comfort, along with an array of perfumes, shawls, and cosmetics. Every morning, the *pujari* explained to me, when the temple is unlocked, the bedsheets are found in disarray and the cosmetics sometimes used.

Vrindivan has so many sacred places where Krishna's childhood *lila* unfolded—a *ghat* where a serpent demon was vanquished; the tree in which He hid, having stolen the bathing *gopis' saris*; a lake where he breathed in and extinguished a raging forest fire. The *ghats* along the Yamuna River are lined with exquisite, dilapidated, red sandstone palaces, with arched colonnades that pilgrims pass through on their circumambulation of the town. In contrast to the jumbling maze and business of Vrindivan, the area just across the Yamuna is an idyllic pastoral landscape of some beauty. Upstream, past lovely green meadowland, is the ashram of Devraha Baba—a modern-style circular tower, simple and white, surrounded by a walkway. Glass windows preserve the saint's hut and few possessions. It is a deeply serene environment with flowering gardens and the occasional peacock.

Many celebrated masters have spent time in Vrindivan. Sri Ramakrishna loved it so much that he could not bear to leave, and only did so after taking a handful of earth and a cutting from a creeper so he could create his own Vrindivan at Dakshineswar just outside of Calcutta where he generally resided. Anandamayee Ma had a Vrindivan ashram, which she would visit as her *keyala* dictated. The place is as tranquil as her ashram in Haridwar, and just across the road is a magnificent Ramakrishna temple *cum* monastery.

The living presence of both of these great masters is exceptionally palpable in their respective shrines; the *pujas* held every evening are most evocative. Sitting in front of the *murti* of Sri Ramakrishna I felt I was sitting in the graceful company of the guru, being showered with his blessing. The definite spiritual empowerment of statues and the transmission of grace radiated by them is one of the real wonders of the Indian

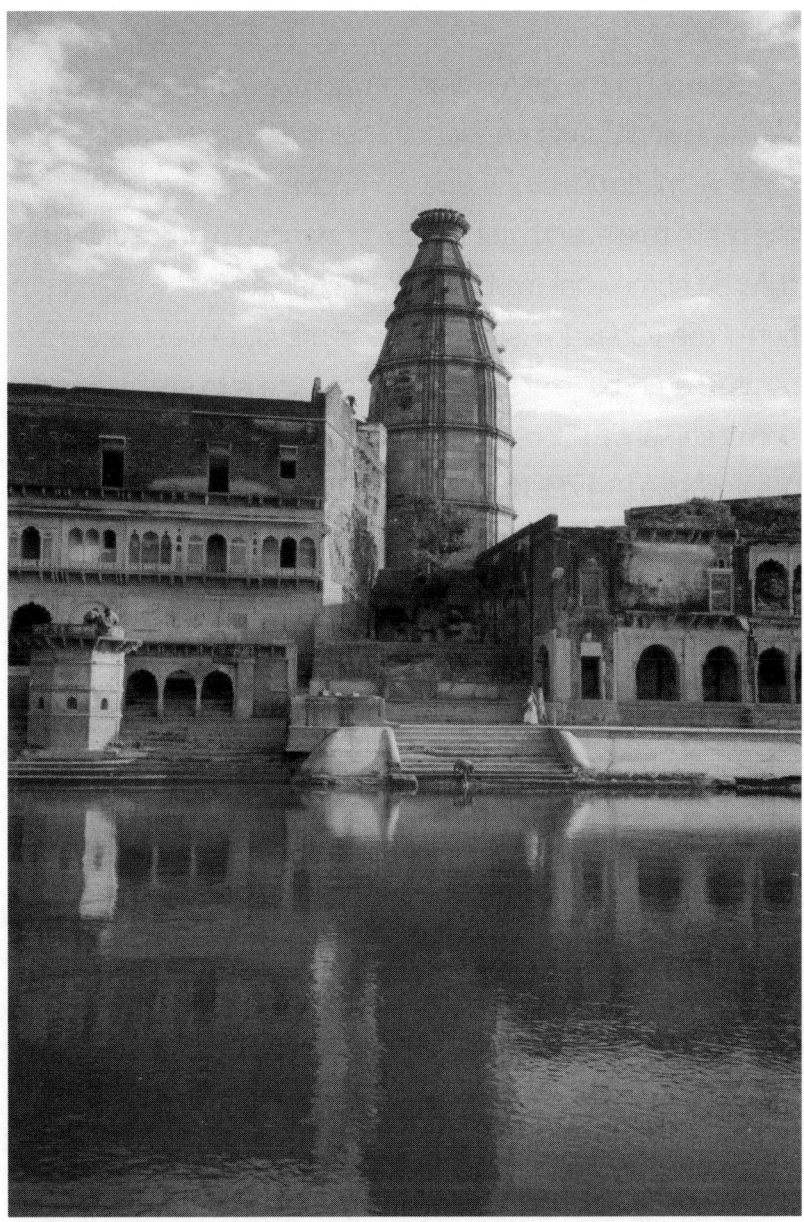

Vrindivan, the childhood home of Krishna, seen from the sacred Yamuna river. The towering central temple, Madana-Mohana, was erected in 1580, and has been a site of worship since then.

spiritual tradition.

Several of the great Vaishnavite *acharyas*—Ramanuja, Vallabha and Chaitanya—whose spiritual lineage continues to this day, made the pilgrimage to Vrindivan. Ramanuja, active in the tenth to eleventh centuries, professed a philosophy that differed somewhat from Shankaracharya's in the interpretation of the *Vedas*. In Ramanuja's and mostly all Vaishnavite systems, the purpose of all spiritual discipline is to attain the position of servant to God, both here and hereafter.

Vallabha (1479-1532) was a child prodigy who was proficient in the *Vedas* and many philosophies before the age of eleven. Vallabha traveled throughout India expounding his doctrine of surrender to God via grace. His cool and scholarly temperament marks him somewhat apart from that great ecstatic, Sri Chaitanya. Chaitanya and Vallabha met in Vrindivan, probably on several occasions. Unfortunately, the schools that formed around them record differing versions of the outcome of those meetings. Colored by sectarian motives, each group of followers seeks to portray their own *acharya* as having outmatched the other in debate.

Sri Chaitanya (1486-1533) is believed by devotees to have been an incarnation of Radha and Krishna in one body. Although a brilliant intellectual, he had to give up his professorship, as, whenever he began teaching, Krishna would appear before him, plunging Nimai, as he was then known, into various states of mystical absorption. Chaitanya went on to become a great saint.

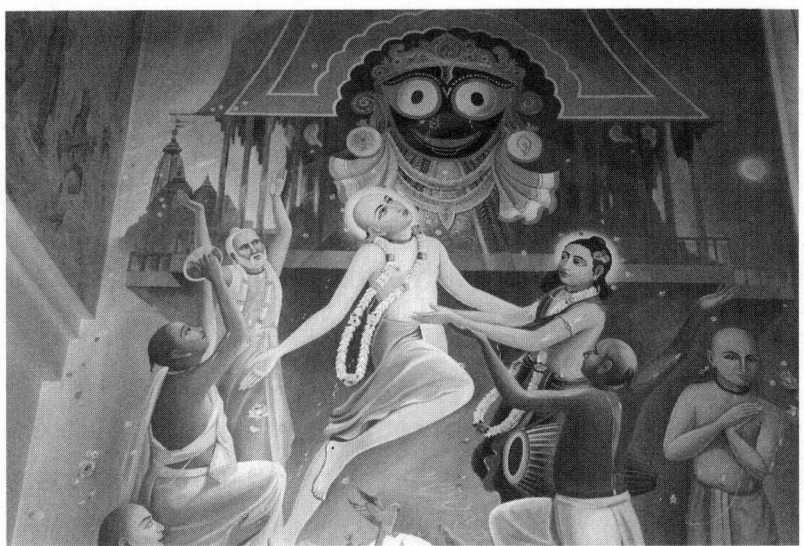

A temple mural in Vrindivan depicts Sri Chaitanya Mahaprabhu dancing in ecstasy.

He instituted the singing of *kirtan* in large groups as an important expression of *bhakti,* and many hostile elements were converted at his touch. He traveled India spreading surrender to Krishna via the frenzied devotional fervor that would escalate into ecstatic absorption as he sang Krishna's name.

Caste and scholarship were unnecessary elements in Chaitanya's teaching, the only qualification being the aspiration to love and serve Krishna. Chaitanya was so enamored of the Yamuna River at Vrindivan that he felt impelled to hurl himself into it. After several rescues, his worried devotees persuaded him to leave the area after only a few months.

Chaitanya was instrumental in the redevelopment of Vrindivan as a site of great spiritual significance. The various sites associated with Krishna's childhood *lila* had become over-grown and lost. He reidentified those places and had two of his closest disciples—the brothers Rupa and Sanatana Gosvami—restore them. They stayed in Vrindivan practicing austerities, meditation, and performing *bhajans*, as well as establishing Sri Chaitanya's teachings through written texts. The brothers were joined by Raghunatha Das, Raghunatha Bhatta, Gopala Bhatta and their nephew Jiva Gosvami—a group that became known as the six Gosvamis. Stories of their learning and spiritual disposition spread far and wide, and earned them the patronage of the Emperor Akbar. Akbar was so impressed with Vrindivan and the Gosvamis that he financed the construction of four great temples there. Sadly, a century later these were later desecrated on the orders of Emperor Aurangzeb. Govindaji temple is still extremely impressive despite the fact that Aurangzeb's troops dismantled the top four floors—the emperor, it seems, was upset that the temple was higher than any mosque in the area. The *samadhi* sites of the Gosvamis are preserved, as are the *bhajan kutirs* of Sanatana and Rupa Gosvami.

Mirabai was another fifteenth-century resident of Vrindivan, and a temple is built where she lived and performed *bhajan*. Mira was a Rajput princess who faced social disgrace and risked her life by refusing to consummate her marriage to a Rajput prince, and by publicly declaring that Krishna was her only Lord and husband. Consequently Mira was hated by the rulers and loved by the people, particularly the most marginalized mem-

bers of society, the *dalit* untouchables. She composed numerous heart-rending songs to Krishna, which are still massively
popular today, and wandered the pilgrim paths clad in the white
cloth of a widow, an *ektara* in her hand. Mirabai is said to have
met her end by merging into a *murti* of Lord Krishna at Dwarka,
just as two emissaries from the ruler of her state waited outside the temple, having been ordered to return Mira to the royal
circle. Alternatively, another theory (also given to explain Sri
Chaitanya's disappearance into a *murti* at Puri), is that she was
murdered within the temple walls by the power brokers of her
day—distressing, but perhaps not surprising, given the fierce
patriarchal values of the proud establishment.

The Hare Krishna movement is extremely active in Vrindivan,
and has a elaborate white marble temple here, of some archi-
tectural achievement. At this temple I encountered the next
interviewee, Rajasekhara dasa Brahmacari, who was immediately enthusiastic about this project. He has a gift for oratory
and is clearly well used to public speaking and debate; in fact,
he spoke so touchingly about his master, Srila Prabhupada, that
I had to wipe tears from my eyes. Rajasekhara dasa Brahmacari
represents the orthodox Gaudiya Vaishnava tradition, and
around him I sensed a certain kind of power that comes from
absolute personal conviction over one's beliefs. Not without
humor, he elucidated the complex Gaudiya theology with both
ease and flair.

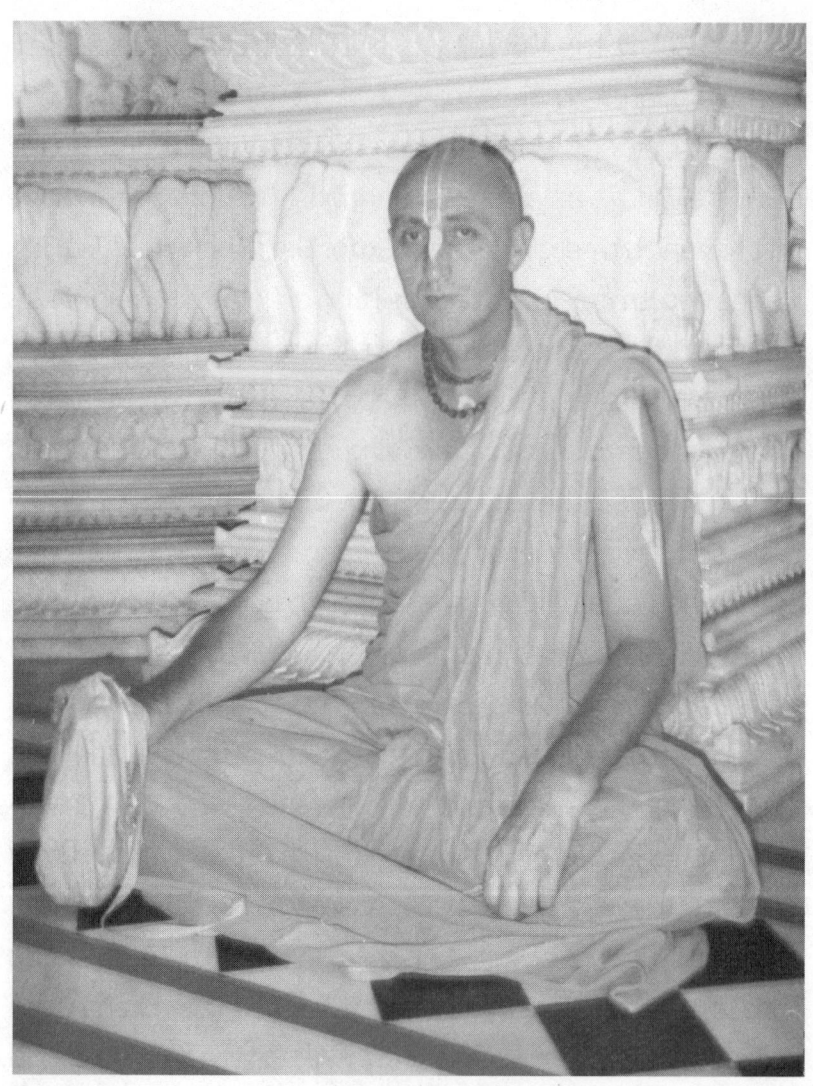

Rajasekhara Dasa Brahmacari

## Rajasekhara Dasa Brahmacari

I am from Salisbury in England. Childhood was very miserable. I felt there was something wrong with life—it wasn't the bed of roses it was supposed to be. At school I had a natural appetite for religion and history, but little interest in academic pursuit. I wasn't interested in a career—even though my parents wanted me to take care of the future, the future did not interest me. I wanted to know about the present.

When I left school the Beatles were very popular, and by the time I was seventeen or eighteen the hippie movement had started. There was definitely a spiritual side to that in the beginning. They knew God was there somewhere, and searched for alternatives—the anti-establishment ethos.

From the age of five I'd had a nightmare that I was going to die and that beyond death there was just a black void. It frightened me very much.

I couldn't comprehend life—a wife, children, possessions and then it's all gone? What kind of life is this? So from age five I wanted to find the answer to death, which was also the answer to life. During that hippie period I began to deeply search for God, and I started studying all types of scriptures to try to understand the truth of life, its purpose, and who had created it. I did a deep study of the New Testament to try to understand the life of Jesus. Still, it was unclear; there was no clear conception of God—just an invisible entity with no description of His world, form, or qualities. So, still I was unsatisfied. Then I came to Buddhist scriptures; the life of the Buddha immediately attracted me. It was practical to renounce the material world and take the life of a mendicant. Buddha had everything—a beautiful wife, opulence, even a newborn child, but he had achieved a certain level of enlightenment that allowed him to renounce in an instant.

I started doing six hours of *hatha* yoga a day and became vegetarian. Around this time I came into contact with some magazines from the Hare Krishna movement, and for the first time in my life I saw that there were other people doing something practical for their spiritual evolution. It seemed similar to Buddhism, but I could see there was a very joyful and blissful aspect to their spiritual practices. When I saw a picture of their master—Bhaktivedanta Srila Prabhupada, I felt that this man had no false ego. In Buddhism, to see how the ego works and to conquer it is very important. I'd observed the male ego, and I saw in Srila Prabhupada's face this peaceful mood of someone who is free of the influence of false ego.

I found the language of the movement very difficult to comprehend, but the spiritual master and the joyous mood on the faces of the devotees very much attracted me. Around this same time the Hare Krishna *mantra* had become a big hit in the pop charts. For many years when I was a hippie, in my so-called "trances" or under the influence of cannabis, I would hear this music. Sometimes from the rocks on the beach I would hear transcendental music.

One day I was in my mother's kitchen with the radio on and suddenly I heard this same music—I couldn't quite believe it! I went over to the radio and heard that it was the Hare Krishna *mantra* sung by the Radha Krishna temple—it was the same music I'd been hearing for years! A few weeks later I went into town and heard it being played live. The hairs on my body stood up and I started to feel this very ecstatic feeling I'd not had before. I looked out of the window of the bus I was on and there I saw a group of Hare Krishna devotees chanting, beating drums, and banging symbols. They were all dressed in robes of Indian origin, with shaven heads and yellow *tilak* markings on their foreheads. So different! They were effulgent and joyful! I thought, "This is the life for me."

My brother opened a boutique and started selling incense manufactured by the devotees—so we had contact with them. I went off to Greece on a vacation to see a little of the world, but I ran out of money and hitchhiked around. Feeling miserable I started chanting the Hare Krishna *mantra*. This gave me strength and solace, so I returned back to England with the feeling that I had to join the movement. There was nothing else in life worth doing for me other than to become a yogi. Of course, I still had some reservations and went to stay with my brother. Coincidentally, he had invited a group of Hare Krishna devotees to come and stay with him a few days. The first devotee arrived and when he explained to me the yoga of *bhakti,* devotion to Krishna, I became totally convinced there was no other life for me than to become a devotee of Krishna.

The other devotees came and we had ecstatic *kirtans* every morning and evening. When they left I also left with them, and went to join the movement in Manchester. I felt I had been reborn and was in another world—safe, secure, happy, and peaceful. I felt completely fulfilled to have taken shelter at the lotus feet of Sri Krishna. I felt all my material anxieties had finished, and there was a new life ahead. I was twenty-two years old. That was November 1972. By March I had been asked to transfer to a new temple, a large country estate in a small village, donated by George Harrison of the Beatles.

Even though I'd not been formally initiated, my managerial abilities had been recognized and I'd been made the temple commander. George Harrison came there a few times; he was a very happy person, dedicated to serving Krishna. That house had cost three quarters of a million pounds and he just gave it to Bhaktivedanta Srila Prabhupada, who he loved very much. In fact, George wanted to shave up and become a Hare Krishna devotee, but Srila Prabhupada told him: "You are a Beatle, you should remain a Beatle, simply sing songs for Krishna. And try to serve in whichever way you can, and in this way Krishna will bless you." He did a very great service to the movement. From the time he started to release their songs, the movement took off in a very big way in the world.

On the birthday of Srila Prabhupada's spiritual master, George sent a Rolls Royce full of roses as an offering. Srila Prabhupada was very moved and blessed him that he would go back to Krishna in this life. I was at the manor and we were redecorating, waiting for the master's first visit to this new temple. When the day arrived he came by helicopter; we were all waiting when he descended and stepped out onto the lawn. We all burst into tears. This was the effect of seeing him—it was very moving. One has to experience such phenomena for oneself. On seeing his face and humble demeanor my realization was, "This is my eternal spiritual father." As he walked into the dark hall of the manor his effulgence illuminated the whole area like a shining light: never before had I seen such a personality. We were very lucky; he stayed for many weeks, writing, lecturing, and meeting important people.

I had the privilege of escorting him from his room to the lecture hall. I'd hand him his cane—he was an elderly gentleman, over seventy. I'd place his slippers on his feet and guide him down the stairs to the temple. Afterwards I'd do the same, escorting him back to his quarters. I felt this was the perfection of life, to be able to touch the lotus feet of a pure devotee of the Lord and to render the most menial services. I still feel, after twenty years of being a devotee, that this was the best service I'd done.

Everyone who met Srila Prabhupada loved him; it was a very wonderful phenomenon that he could evoke such feelings in our hearts. His profound knowledge of spiritual life and of the sacred *Vedic* scriptures was unfathomable. He could quote verbatim over seven thousand *slokas* from the *Vedas*.

At that time British people did not need visas for India, and Srila Prabhupada felt it would be good for the British devotees to go there as the Americans could not stay long. So, in 1975 I decided I would go to India—into the holy land of Vrindivan, about which I'd heard so much. According to our beliefs, Vrindivan is not part of the material world, rather it is like an oasis—a part of Vaikuntha's atmosphere here; a direct replica of the spiritual world where Krishna lives eternally.

When I first came here the construction of a beautiful temple was in full swing; everyone was working very hard. On arrival in India I was surprised to see people in Western clothing, with cars, and tall buildings, I wasn't expecting that! Still, wherever you go in India it is like a carnival—cows, dogs, noise, hogs, people, monkeys, asses, music, smells of Indian cooking, incense fragrances permeating the air. I felt very happy to be in India, I felt this is home. The people are wonderful and don't look so miserable, drawn, and frustrated as Western people generally do.

The children laugh and smile; people are ready to talk and greet you. Even the beggars are happy. Not like in England where people don't even look at each other! India was a place where one could live as a *sadhu*, dress as a *sadhu*, and be respected as a *sadhu*. One did not have to hide one's appearance for fear of being abused, as was being done in England. It's a place where people respect those who have renounced the world to serve the lotus feet of the Supreme Lord.

After one month in Vrindivan I went to visit the world head-quarters of the movement in Nevadweap Dharma, one hundred miles north of Calcutta. I was trained in how to worship the deity in the *sanctum sanctorum* so that I could return to Vrindivan, when the temple opened, and be one of the first *pujaris* there. Srila Prabhupada came for the opening in April 1975; we were very fortunate to get a lot of his association. After some time serving in the temple I went traveling with devotees—holding programs, conducting festivals, chanting, distributing books and *prasadum*. This I did for many years. Wherever we went in India we were warmly received. India is a place where one becomes very conversant with *Vedic* philosophy because everyone here knows something about the philosophy. Even a common rickshaw driver has more spiritual knowledge than the President of the United States of America does.

Practically every Indian understands the law of *karma*—for every action a reaction. Practically every Indian understands about rebirth and the laws of reincarnation, and that the desire of living entities causes them to be born again to fulfil these same desires. Only when the material desires have been purified and there is no more desire to enjoy sense gratification in the material world can one become liberated from repeated birth and death. Our master used to say that every Indian is a devotee, but due to the bad effects of the *Kali Yuga* they are fallen and have been captured by the illusory energy of *maya*. They have now turned away from their original *sanatana dharma* and are striving to imitate the West. He said that bringing his disciples from the West would surprise the Indians—"How is it these Westerners have given up all these wonderful things we are so eager to enjoy?" In this way we can convince the Indians that the ways of the West are not only temporary and fleeting pleasures, but that they also lead to great suffering.

India is a special land. This particular land is known as Bharat Varsha or Tapa Bhumi—this means renunciation land, the land of renunciation. For us the most important place in India is Vrindivan, where Krishna appeared to take birth. (Understanding that he has not taken birth, but appeared in his original transcendental form.) The other important holy places to us are Badrinath, Dwarka, Puri, and Rameshwaram—these are holy *dhams,* a place that is a part of the spiritual world rather than then material.

In India, God Himself has walked besides many thousands and thousands of *rishis,* yogis, sages and *mahatmas.* These great saintly personalities have performed great austerities and many sacrifices for the benefit of those who want to advance on the path of yoga. This is one of the reasons why India is such an important place, not only in this world, but also within the whole universe. Here, incarnations of God appear and give their teachings to the whole world.

Five hundred years ago, Sri Chaitanya Mahaprabhu appeared—Krishna Himself appearing in the form of a devotee. He inaugurated the process of chanting the *maha mantra: Hare Krishna Hare Krishna Krishna Krishna Hare Hare, Hare Rama Hare Rama Rama Rama Hare Hare.* It has been declared in the *Vedic* scripture that this is a great chant for deliverance in the age of *Kali Yuga.*

Lord Chaitanya took *sannyas* at the early age of twenty-four, and traveled all over India spreading the chanting of the holy name. He declared that for all those who are born in India, their prime duty is to understand the science of God, and in turn, go all over the world to preach to all humanity. Srila Prabhupada was one of the few Indians who took up this mission, and by his sincere service was able to spread this *mantra* all over the face of the planet. Even today, in the highest reaches of the Himalayas, many thousands of *rishis* and yogis perform austerities for the benefit of the people of the world. This is the real purpose of India.

Yoga means to link with God. The English word "yoke" is born from this word yoga. Just as a yoke is used to connect two buckets, yoga is the instrument for connecting two souls—the *jiva* soul and the Supreme soul. This is India's gift to the world, and those who come here can dive deep into this sublime process of God realization.

Those people who visit India are not ordinary people, they do not have ordinary *karma,* they have special *karma.* By coming to India the effect of the sacred land will change their lives. Those who then visit holy places are the most fortunate of all—because it says in the scriptures one who visits the holy *dham* will not take birth in this world again.

In the course of writing books on Vrindivan I have been very fortunate to be able to research the history of this sacred place, to visit the most important of the five thousand temples here, and to associate with the local people who are all devotees of Krishna. It has given me greater insight into spiritual India. India *means* spirituality, and without it there is no meaning to India. India holds the greatest beauty, the greatest knowledge, the greatest philosophy, the greatest people, the greatest saints, and the greatest opportunity to achieve the goal of human life.

I went back to the West in 1986 after having been sick in India. It was taking a long time to recover my health so a friend offered me a plane ticket to get good medical facilities. This was the first time I had returned in twelve years, and it seemed almost alien. I could not recognize any car I had seen previously, everything had changed so much due to the rapid advancement of technologies.

On driving from the airport to central London I was amazed

to see no one on the streets, unlike India, where the streets are packed solid from morning to night. I missed that festival of humanity. I remember one morning catching the bus to the hospital; I sat at the back on the upper-deck as people got on. I noticed that each and every one of them looked like hell. They were all on their way to work; nobody smiled or greeted one another to pass the time of day. They all appeared to be dreading another day in their lives.

Even though they have so many facilities for sense enjoyment—television, theatres, cinemas, bars, many varieties of cigarettes, alcohol, intoxicants of various types—nonetheless here I was seeing first-hand that when they wake up in the morning they look like death. These things may temporarily satisfy the senses, but they do not satisfy the inner self—this is why these people looked so miserable. Just like if one has a parrot in a cage; if one polishes, clean, and maintains the cage very nicely, but forgets to feed the parrot inside, the parrot will die. So, Western civilization is very expert in polishing the cage, but they have absolutely no knowledge of how to feed the bird inside the cage. In other words, they have no idea of how to satisfy the spirit soul trapped within the body—though being expert in looking after the body.

In the West people are so much brainwashed by television, advertising, hoarding everywhere encouraging mindless sense-gratification—simply like cattle being herded to the slaughterhouse with no knowledge that they are being led to their death.

In India millions of people are aware of the difference between the body and soul, and we find millions of people engaged in caring for the soul rather than only caring for the body. This is what the West must learn, and only India can teach this to them. In India even the homeless have beautiful faces, and a certain peace and contentment about them, a certain faith in God that generally cannot be found in the West.

We in the Hare Krishna movement are eternally indebted to our beloved spiritual master for having taken the trouble at such an advanced age to come to the West to teach the glories of Vedic culture.

## 11

Behind the Hare Krishna's Krishna Balarama Mandir (temple, or shrine) is a small suburb known as the Madhuvan colony where several Western devotees of Radha Krishna live. There I met Bhamini Sharan on the back of a motorbike he was driving—a friend of his was eager for me to meet their spiritual master, Sri Sri 108 Sri Ananda Vibhuset, and Bhamini gave me a lift. His guru was self-effacing, and perhaps even a little shy. He sweetly invited me in to see his *thakerjee*, which it turned out was a small attractive painting of Radha Krishna.

Devotional practices of the Nimbarki sect center around these images, which are considered as none other than the living deities, Radha Krishna. I watched as he carefully adjusted a miniature blanket wrapped around the image, and moved a heater around, to keep the deities warm! The guru administered to their perceived needs as a doting mother would tend to an adored infant.

In the Vaishnava path, a mood of pure, soft, and gentle sentiment accompanies the intimate relationship with the form of the Divine. The deity may be perceived as one's child, friend, brother, master, or lover. (It feels very innocent and sweet.) In Rajasthan, the worship of one's personal deity has reached such a level that many women spend all their time preparing special dishes to offer their *thakerjee*—that means breakfast, lunch, dinner, supper, and choice snacks every day. In fact, their homes are considered to belong to their *thakerjee*, and themselves servants within it. Goodness knows what kind of overdrive these ladies go into at celebration times!

Later, I spoke to Bhamini on a warm balcony as the sun set over Vrindivan.

## Bhamini Sharan

Nineteen years ago I passed through one of the international organizations established for worshipping Krishna; this was in Amsterdam. I stayed for twelve years as a *brahmacharya* serving in the Amsterdam temple and opening some further branches. Mainly I was preaching their gospel and teachings.

I became a little disillusioned by what I saw as the money-mindedness of the situation, and found that I had been involved long enough. I wanted a similar but different form of spiritual life—something more devotional, and from my heart. So, I came to India to tour various holy places. I settled in Vrindivan with my wife and her mother, who later died here. We visited various *mahatmas,* and one day while I was building our place here I passed through the stool field—where people go to pass stool. I met my guru there! I greeted him and felt there was something very special about him. Later I met him again. He spoke in such a familiar way about Radha Rani that I felt he was an embodiment of Radha Rani.

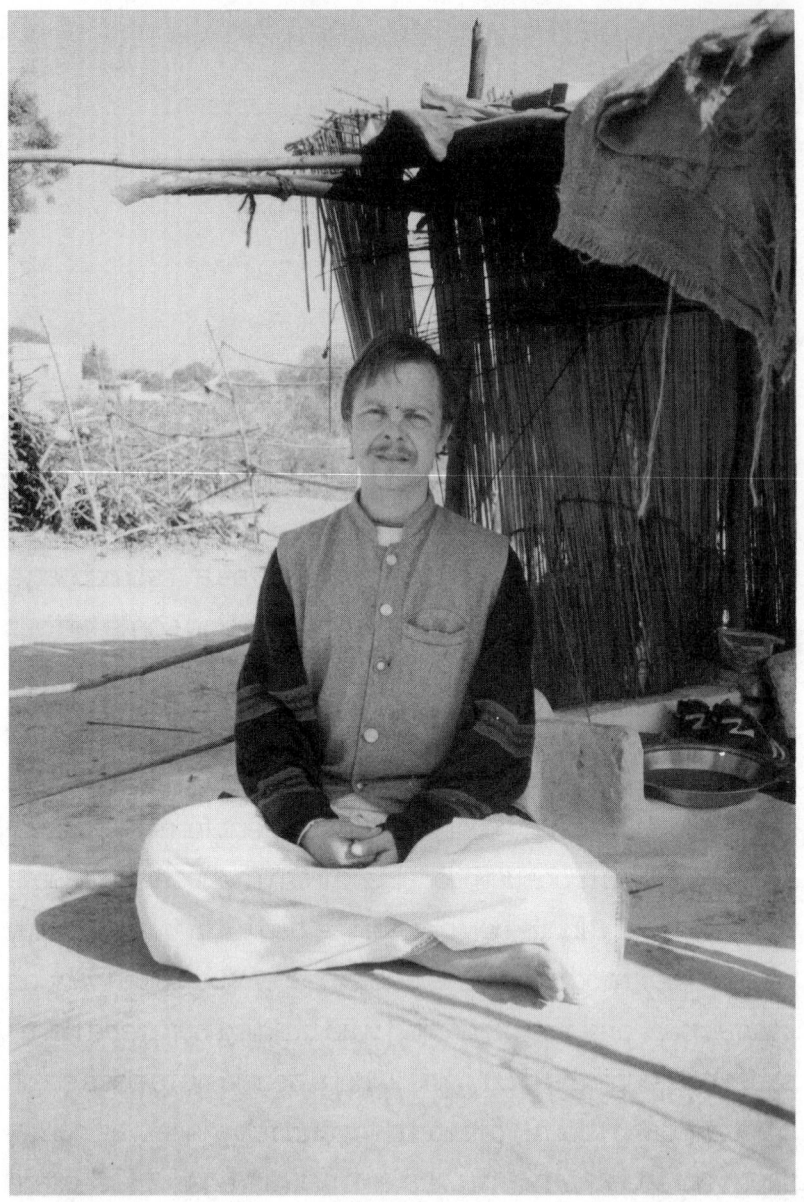

Bhamini Sharan

I was interested, so he said I could come and listen to Braj
*lilas* describing the divine pastimes of Radha and Krishna and
their intimate associates. When we questioned him if he could
teach us *bhajan* and give us initiation, he said it was only possible if we lived in Vrindivan and joined the *sampradaya,* the
lineage he belonged to. My guru's name is Sri Sri 108 Sri Ananda
Vibhuset, which means "one who is decorated with unlimited
spiritual ornaments." The lineage is known as the Sri Hans
Sampradaya, or nowadays, Sri Nimbark Sampradaya.

There have been obstacles to our staying on here. Once we
were nearly beaten to death by robbers who fractured my skull.
Still, we decided to stay, attracted by the colors and fragrance
that surrounds this beautiful environment.

The *sadhana* we practice is known as *mansik madhana,*
which is meditating on different parts of Krishna's *lila* in the
mood of female accompaniment of Radha Krishna—this is called
*Rasupasana.* We take the name of the Lord Radha Krishna,
and this is the beginning—to contemplate on the name. There
is also the *Mahavani,* a book we study that is considered to be
the embodiment of all Vrindivan in one book. There is an inner
meaning to it, which can only be explained by a real guru; we
consider it to be the quintessence of all Vaishnavite writing. It
describes the portions of a day of Radha Krishna, and whatever is within that; the seasons, the activities, and inner, cherished, loving emotions. We have learned it in our hearts and
recite the prayers in original Vrindivan language. Whatever the

*sloka* describes, that we meditate on. We do not see Radha as
being a servant of Krishna; we see them as indivisible. They are
the Source.

According to our philosophy, we believe that the various
*sampradayas* manifest in different *yugas*. Ours manifested during the *satya yuga*. On the banks of the Yamuna River in Vrindivan
there were four saints, in children's bodies, known as the
*sankardi rishis*—they were visited by Hans Bhagavan, Radha
Krishna incarnated in the body of a swan. Hans Bhagavan initiated them into the Gopal *mantra*. There was a conversation,
and at the end of it a tear fell from Hans Bhagavan's eye. It was
a tiny stone, and he said he was embodied in this *salagram*
stone, that this embodies Radha Krishna. This *salagram* has
stayed as an item of worship for the entire *yugas* up until now,
passed on through a lineage of saints, and presently cared for
by our *acharyas*.

We feel that Vrindivan is the eternal residence of God, where
God is always at home, where God is normal and as Himself—
playful, loving, and sweet. God at home is Krishna in Vrindivan.
Krishna says that He never goes one step outside of Vrindivan.
When Krishna appeared five thousand years ago he went to
Dwaraka for most of his life, but in a subtle form his heart and
being were always here, and the *gopis* were aware of that.
Though they were always feeling separation, He was still per-
sonally present, but not visible to all eyes. It depends on the
*bhav* one holds in one's heart. Krishna only likes love; anything

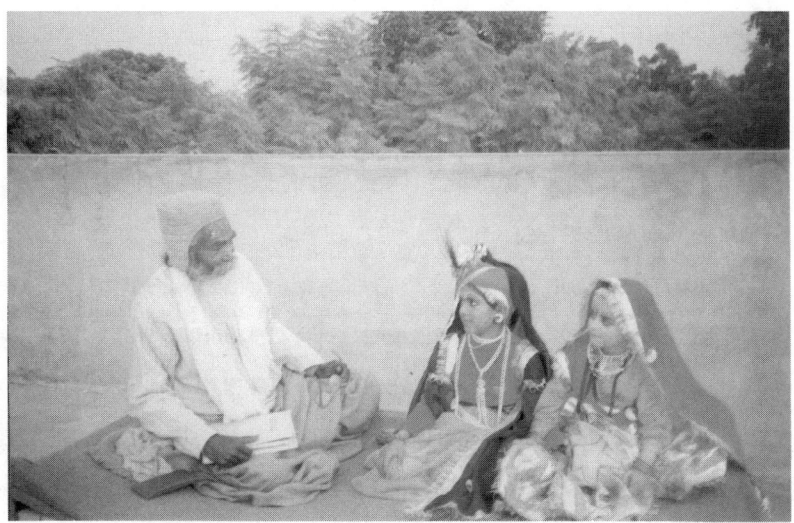

Sri Sri 108 Sri Ananda Vibuhset, with children dressed as Radha and Krishna.

prepared with love He accepts.

Having been a devotee already, there was an intimacy that enabled me to accept all of Vrindivan—the salty water, pigs, thorny trees, the dirt. People who are overly materialistic do not like to stay here, but *sadhus* cannot leave this place. When Krishna incarnated here, all of the other gods are said to have incarnated too, to enjoy and witness the activities of the Lord in that form. Therefore, it is said that a *sadhu* need not go on pilgrimage to any other place. The importance is not the external but the internal—there is a very pure vibration going all the time. There is so much beauty here. Vrinda is the flower architect of Vrindivan, and flowers are present at all times of the year. In summer here, when it is very hot, the temples have cooling water-springs and are fully adorned with flowers—like flower bungalows. When it is cold, they put gloves and warm blankets on the deities and offer them warming food. Krishna is our soul, and everything is service to Him. There can be no philosophizing or fighting because everyone is seen as part of Krishna; no one is less, no one is more.

I cannot exist in the West so easily as it is so commercialized that it feels as though people have lost their souls. Money has become "god" and rules people's lives and values; human values have been lost. There was once a *mahatma* here named Bhagavat Rasik who said that if a *sadhu* touches money he becomes turned away from Krishna and guru. It is not a matter of touching it with the hands; it is a matter of touching it with the heart. There should be, eventually, no greed in the heart. Even if a real *sadhu* sits in an opulent position he is completely detached. Things come and go. In any situation, a *sadhu* should be satisfied. He should only accept what is offered in love and devotion. Those of us who have taken birth in the Western world should quickly see through it. Let people become loving and sweet—there is treasure in that.

Sri Chitanya Mahaprabhu was a force that came to unite beings—not to create a sect that would consider itself supreme. People should not be sectarian, but sadly there is a great deal of sectarianism in contemporary Vaishnavism.

Chaitanya Mahaprabhu took initiation from Iswara Puri in the Vaishnava *sampradaya*. But to show others not to be sectarian he also took initiation from the *sampradaya* of

Shankaracharya, the great exponent of Advaita Vedanta. Within that order he even took initiation into one of the lower orders to show the initiates into the highest order—the Saraswati order— not to be proud. He purposely humiliated the orthodox Vaishnavas by doing this. He was there to unite Hindu *dharma*, and by his devotion he embraced all the different forms.

One should always see others as a part of God. A genuine heart should be established in the *sadhaka*.

## 12

Along Vrindivan's *parikrama* path, in a lane filled with ashrams and temples, is the ashram of Neem Keroli Baba. It was here that he took *maha samadhi* in 1973. Neem Keroli Baba is revered over much of northern India as a miraculous saint with a manner as gruff as it was tender. His insults were a famous blessing! Maharaji, as devotees knew him, was regarded as an incarnation of Hanuman, the monkey God and hero of the Ramayana, and at all of his ashrams there are *mandirs* dedicated to this supreme servant of Rama, and a strong *bhava* of Hanuman *bhakti*. At the verdant Rishikesh *ashram* there is a glorious fifty-foot high Hanuman built on top of a room where Neem Keroli Baba would sit. The atmosphere inside that tiny cell is exceptionally still and full of remembrance. In Vrindivan the Hanuman *murti* is smaller but equally powerful, and accompanied by pristine shrines to the goddess Durga, and to Rama and Sita. In the Rama-Sita *mandir*, as instructed by Maharaji, ladies known as *bhajan mas* continuously chant the names of God. Morning and evening *pujas* are performed in turn at each shrine, climaxing with the circumambulating of the *samadhi* tomb.

One can enter the room where Neem Keroli Baba stayed and sit by his tucket, which is covered with one of his characteristic brown plaid blankets. Devotees quietly enter the cool room and reverentially place their hands or foreheads against the feet of a life-size photograph of Maharaji reclining on that same tucket.

I met Mr. K. Das at the ashram, and it was wonderful to be able to speak with someone who had spent so long with Neem Keroli Baba, given the fact that the saint was discovered by Westerners at a fairly late stage in his life, and was fond of sending them away once they had found him! Mr. K. Das talked about his guru straight from his heart, and touched me with his affable and humble demeanor.

# Mr. K. Das

I had absolutely no knowledge about India or Hinduism until
I reached here . . . absolutely zero. I was brought up a Roman
Catholic, with all that image worship and ritualistic stuff. I
reached India on New Year's Eve, 1970, at twenty-two years
old. It was just another place. I had no destination—all I knew
about India was that it was a great destination for hippies. The
first place I went to was Hampi in south India, which is nothing
like Hampi today—there were no *bhang lassi* shops. Now it's a
major dope destination.

I met a wandering *sadhu* who lived on the banks of the
sacred river there; I didn't know what a *sadhu* was. I lived with
him for two weeks wandering the area—this was my first exposure to a holy man or an ascetic. I found my way to Benares
where I stayed put for three months living on a houseboat during the monsoon. I got my hands on books about Hinduism,
meditation, and yoga—things like that. Then it was on to
Uttarakhand in the Himalayas. Any additional plan I had of just

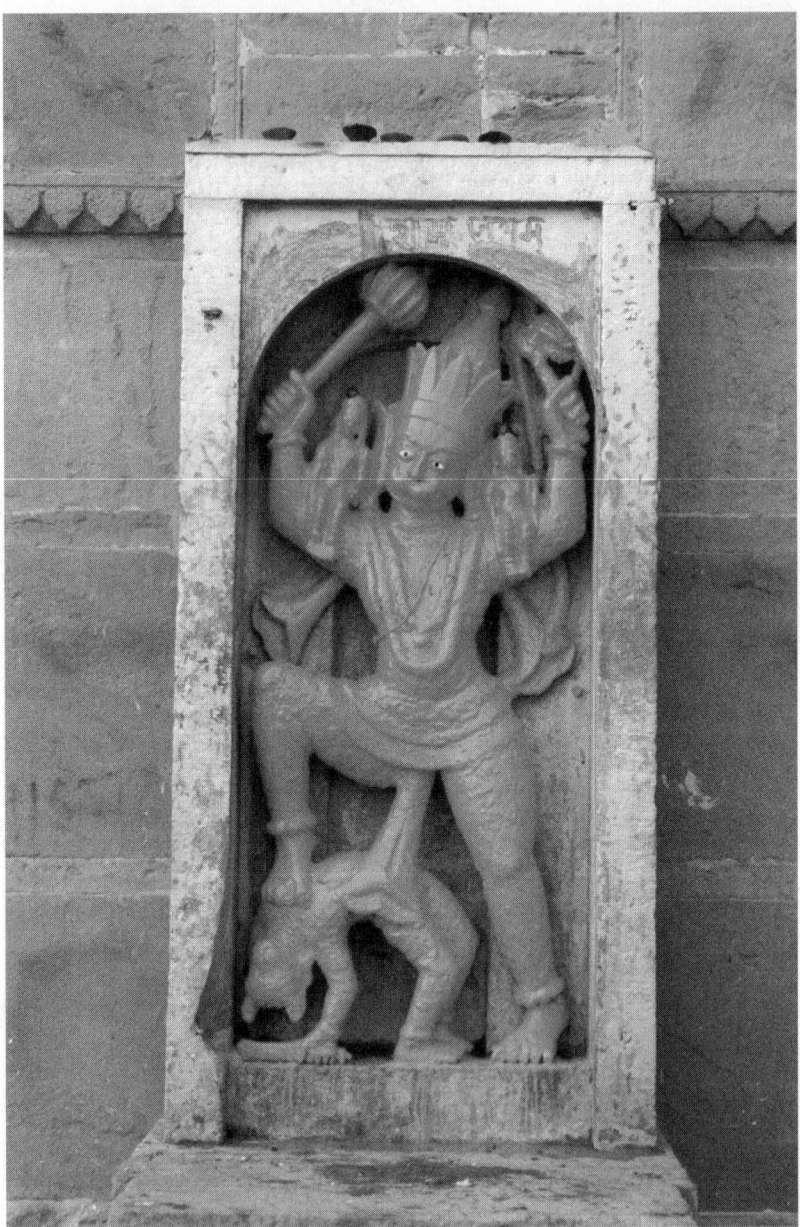

Hanuman
Devotees of Neem Keroli Baba believed him to be an incarnation of Hanuman, the servant of Lord Rama, whose exploits are described in the Hindu epic the *Ramayana*.

treating India as a place on my world tour disappeared. I had no desire to go anywhere else.

I lived in a waterless, electricity-less hut in the Himalayas for one year reading the books of Ramakrishna, Vivekananda, Paramahansa Yogananda, classic books on Hinduism, the *Bhagavad Gita*—I was particularly drawn to Advaita Vedanta and Pantanjali yoga.

To get to my hut I had to pass by the ashram of Neem Karoli Baba. This is where I first came across his name. In those days I was unaware that he had any Western followers, nor was I looking to become a follower of anybody. I did visit twice, and each time Maharaji was not there. Some time later I heard from my sister; she was coming to India with the former Harvard professor, Richard Alpert, who was now known as Ram Dass, and fifteen to twenty of his followers. I didn't know who *he* was either. They came to see Neem Karoli Baba and bought with them photos and stories of Maharaji. But, until 1971, Maharaji was not seeing foreigners on any regular basis. If you got to see him it was just "in, and out!"

Six months later they stayed waiting for Maharaji to tell them to come. I got bitten by a snake, and the bite did not heal quickly. Six or seven weeks later I realized I had to get out of my hut and do something about my health, which I had thought would just take care of itself. So I went to Nainital where there was an old British hospital with a good reputation. By chance I arrived for hospitalization on the same day Ram Dass and company—

including my sister—had gotten a message from Maharaji that they could come and see him at his ashram in Nainital district. After a few days of hearing stories from my visitors while I laid around in the hospital—stories of their day having *darshan* of Marharji—I too wanted to have his *darshan.* After five or six days I checked out and was taken by taxi to the ashram, where I met him for the first time.

The initial few days were very powerful, almost as if I was in a trance state. We would spend from eight a.m. 'till five p.m. at the ashram, during which we would have several extended periods in his company. There was an awesome power that emanated from Neem Karoli Baba and it spread hundreds of yards out from him—this enormous spiritual presence. The dominant *rasa* or feeling of this presence was of some kind of extraordinary love. He manifested love. The physical manifestation he showed, to the foreigners at least, was very childlike, loving, and playful; and he treated us like even smaller children. He would answer questions if asked, but only of a spiritual practice nature. (However, the Indians always had personal questions.) His answers were very simple—he did not preach or philosophize; he was absolutely non-dogmatic. There was a common denominator to all his answers. Whether the questions were spiritual or personal his answer always came down to "Remember God, love God." Those were his teachings. If you wanted to do yoga he would send you to Swami Muktananda; if you wanted miracles, to Sathya Sai Baba; or if you wanted meditation, to

184

Goenka at Bodh Gaya.

Often foreigners would come with some kind of background in these things, and they saw that Maharaji was not living up to any of their expectations of what a guru should be. Frequently Westerners would sit in front of him in a pose of meditation, so Maharaji would send a well-aimed banana at their chests to get them to open their eyes and get back with the program.

The Guru is a wish-fulfilling tree, and you can get whatever you want from the guru. Maharji was offering the greatest fruit of all, and if you did not want that he would send you on. His own specialty was love. He was offering everything to everyone.

Words are inadequate to describe the overwhelming feeling of spiritual energy which was packaged in a very sweet and lovely form. This form sometimes gave *darshan* in a wrathful aspect, but generally in a loving and childlike manner. He was like Father God and Child God. The wrathfulness he occasionally manifested seemed to be just another *rupa,* another form, to be used when required. The times I saw him like that it would be directed for some reason, but almost simultaneously he'd be laughing and joking with others.

Maharji had a tremendous power of communication. He would give *darshan* for hours to a continuous stream of Indians and the odd foreigner. Frequently, he had fifty to one hundred people sitting with him, and they all felt that Maharji was paying personal attention to them. He seemed to remember everyone's name, history, and family. People coming for the first time, who had never met him before, would be told by him who they were, where they'd come from, why they'd come to see him, and things about their grandmothers.

He was seen by the Indian devotees to be an incarnation of Hanuman, and his primary teaching, if there is one, is that of *bhakti*. He was a universalist in his views; his favorite saying was *"Sub Ek"*—All is One. He used to say, "Remember God and all things will be okay."

I guess my relationship with him was like a son's. He once kissed me on the head and told me that he was my real father. He put me through lots of paces for the two years I was with him—from the day he opened his doors to foreigners to the day he left his body. The relationship went through all kinds of changes. When I first met him I was the stubborn yogi type—I did not believe you had to do what the guru said, at least the first time he said it. So now, perhaps, I'm less stubborn and a little kinder and softer, though that's hard to say about yourself.

Anyway, he was kind and loving with me, sometimes stern, but mostly sweet and loving, though not always gentle. I think it was like being hypnotized, all you remembered was the hypnotist. All that became important was the hypnotist telling you, "Now you will love God." These things came automatically, as he was not lecturing or teaching in any traditional sense. So, gradually, or for some instantaneously, the power of Maharaji manifested in a constant remembrance of Maharaji. I've been told by other saints I met subsequently that *bhakti* yoga is the

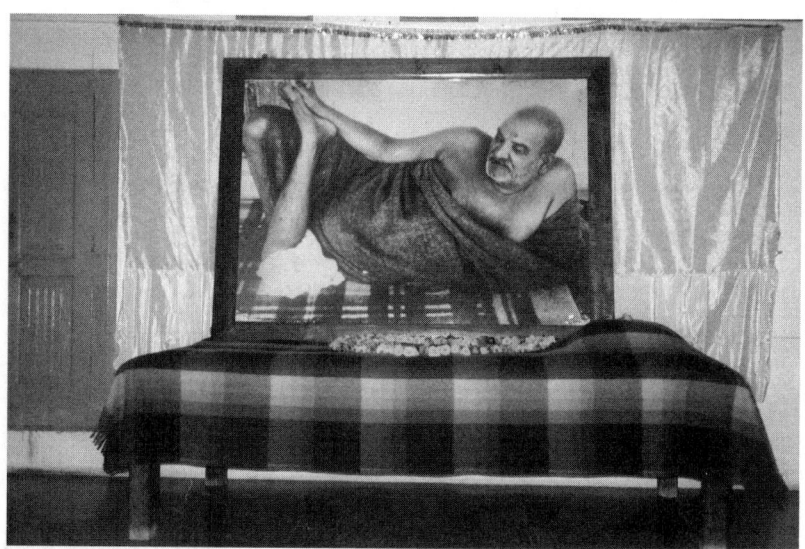

Neem Keroli Baba's photograph on his tucket (daybed).

highest form; all paths eventually lead to *bhakti* yoga; and that the greatest form of this yoga is guru *bhakti*—which is devotion to God in human form. He had us sing a lot.

Many Westerners could not handle the food so Maharaji set up a separate kitchen; there was a lot of *seva* there. He frequently said, as a teaching, "Feed people."

After he left his body I stayed eight or ten months, during which time myself and two others went among Maharaji's devotees collecting stories, which would then become the basis of Ram Dass's book, *The Miracle of Love*. By Marahaji's grace I've never had to hold down a regular job, and he has allowed me to spend half of the last twenty-four years, since he left his body, in India—mostly in his ashrams where, out of our own personal fashion and dim abilities, we go on with what we loosely call the practice of guru *bhakti* yoga, which is the dominant *bhava* of our lives.

My relationship with him has become more internalized since he left the body. The process, which was there from the beginning, accelerated when I saw his lifeless body, and saw that lifeless body cremated. Also, living in his ashrams I was used to the ongoing exposure of externalizing the worship of the guru through statues. I feel there is now an awareness I did not have before of continuity in my relationship to the Guru who for some time had the form of Neem Karoli Baba. I believe that by his grace I have had his *darshan* through two lifetimes.

Neem Karoli Baba lived from 1900 to 1973, and I have the feeling that probably we were old Indians back when he was younger, and that somehow these devotees, in the grand scheme of things, were reborn in the West. Through no great merit or effort on our part we were bought back to his lotus feet—a miracle of love. My relationship to him is a deeply internalized fact, and this relationship happily dominates my life.

Maharji once refused to meet Indira Gandhi when she was travelling to Nainital, and, in fact, left the ashram the day her cavalcade was passing. She was going on a constant tour of India, visiting saints, and anyone she felt had power of some sort, to get them to keep her in power . . . on her side. She had *brahmin* priests throwing things into sacrificial fires twenty-four hours a day! Maharaji was not impressed. One of the things he said was that India would get much worse before it got better, only one in every six houses would hold a light inside. India is a very corrupt place, more corrupt than one could ever imagine. You can't get your post unless you bribe the postman, and he in turn has had to bribe the person within the post office who distributes postal rounds, to get a round in the first place—and so it goes, right to the very top. Corruption has become totally institutionalized. One of the reasons why the streets are so dirty is that there is little real sense of community, outside one's own family and sub-caste. The teachings of the *Bhagavad Gita* are used by the common man to excuse his lack of concern for the state of things, i.e., that good and bad . . . neither really exist, so just do your work. The term "work" has become synonymous with all kinds of corruption—what we may think of as extortion, a person here may think of as work. People drop litter and refuse everywhere, and don't pick it up because it is someone else's job to do that. They paraphrase the *Gita* teaching: "Better to do your own work badly than the work of someone else." The teachings are perverted by the common people, and when applied socially they are a failure, as evidenced by the state of contemporary India. The Kali *yuga* is the human condition. If you read the scriptures that are meant to have taken place in other *yugas* you observe that the same things are happening there—looting, rape, and murder. The *Ashtvakra Gita* describes all of these conditions and responds, "Knowing all of this go about and be happy." Why? Because it provides you with impetus to change and take a path out from that behavior.

In a sense, India does not matter—people will come of their own if they are destined to. If I'm in the West, I live remotely, I don't adopt the general Western lifestyle. Many people who were devotees of Maharaji found themselves living in the West, but not *of* the West. In India there are still places where you can see a lifestyle that is heavily influenced by religion, and in Vrindivan particularly the religion of *bhakti.* You can't see that everywhere, and the person who experiences or witnesses that—it can have a profound impact on their lives.

India is complex, and you cannot generalize. All of India does have a living spiritual tradition, but, at the same time, I know people in the West who never met Neem Karoli Baba—who were born after he died and have no obvious connection with India, other than the fact that the guru was an Indian—who have more love and devotion to him than many of those who have memories of his physical body, and a link to India. Some people need temples and *murtis* and some people don't, so some people need India.

India has freed up spirituality and made it available to all, whereas in the West spirituality has been monopolized by church and state. Our work is whatever we are doing in this moment. In this case it is guru *bhakti.* Everything leads to the sea, it is all the *Ram Lila*—East and West.

# Afterword

India is no longer the place it once was. The increasingly breakneck speed of the people's wholesale appropriation of Western consumerist values has its roots in the British occupation. Her ancient cultural patterns were ignored, derided, and legislated against. A foreign system of education and values enforced. The tragic result has been generations of Western-educated Indians, severely alienated from, and even embarrassed by, the ways of life precious to their forefathers. In common with the rest of Asia, India today is obsessed with imitating the flashy lifestyles of America and Europe. They have bought the lie that happiness and self-worth come from materialistic success. It is a desperate business; even in the slums, satellite dishes blossom—beaming in more of the hypnotic consumerist dream of the "developed" world. In Tiruvannamalai, I witnessed colored televisions being sold within the walls of the sacred Arunacheleswarar temple; a friend remarked, "Where's Jesus when you need him?" Even just a few decades ago, when many of the *sadhus* and *sannyasins* interviewed here arrived, things were different. India offered a general haven for those seeking wisdom, and the power structure was somewhat sympathetic to the Western person's quest. Nowadays, this would be impeded by visa regulations and the erosion of understanding of the value of this lifestyle by the Indian people themselves. Although, having said all of this, perhaps we could learn from the view of an octogenarian *sadhu* I met in Vrindivan. When asked, "Maharaj, you have seen so many changes, has any of this resulted in any good?" He instantly replied, "If everything is Ram's *lila*, who can say what is not good?"

Where spiritual life is most vital is within the company of those few who have woken up to the true nature of Reality. It is exciting and unprecedented that, within the last few decades, we have seen the advent of Western spiritual masters offering the traditional guru-disciple relationship. Through this form we are witnessing the preservation and hopeful flowering of Eastern spiritual culture in the West itself. What was once more or less confined to the East is now, with some investigation, available here also. This organic, natural relationship of transmission and reception is the essence of spiritual life, its root and nourishment. Without it, one is engaged in a guessing game, as pointless as walking through a minefield without a map. Nonetheless, it is specifically this issue—the necessity of the teacher—that Western seekers are generally the most uncomfortable with, and keenest to discredit. This does nothing to dim the primary importance of the guru, as attested to by the experience of hundreds of generations previous to ours, and India's holiest scriptures. One Indian saying puts it plainly: "Guru is God." The danger is the habitual, reductionistic views we are most likely to place on the guru—viewing him or her as a mere personality, though a special one. This, of course, is a major obstacle in optimally utilizing their help.

The sanctity of India could never be totally lost, and we may find its presence in paradoxical situations. In Haridwar there are a string of temples with gaudy fiberglass representations of the principal Hindu pantheon. It is pure theme park kitsch, with fast food available outside. Here I climbed through the artificial caves and plastic forests, past the automated puppet shows, where dusty Ramas and technicolor Sitas enacted a jerky *Ramayana* at the drop of a rupee. Expecting nothing other than more of the same, I came to the climax of this mini-pilgrimage—*darshan* of the temple's deities in the innermost shrine. At once the mood changed, and the merry Hindu holidaymakers around me became silent and serious: we had entered the dark *sanctum sanctorum*. It was a genuine energy found in the more powerful traditional temples. After being blessed by the *pujaris,* we spilled out into the bright sunlight, and I gratefully ate my fast food by a mighty fiberglass Kali, a freshly garroted demon at her feet. A feeling of great relief flooded through me as I reflected, "It can be covered with the most tasteless of forms, but it can never be destroyed—'it' is here!"

God-realized souls will continue to arise in India as they always have. However, those of us drawn to the traditions of *sadhuism* and *sannyas* will be forced to take a more flexible approach, visiting and imbibing what we can, when we can. Unless we are so convinced of our need to reside there that, as I heard of the *sadhu* whose sighting originally inspired this book, we are willing to face imprisonment. Yet, if we should find ourselves within the context of the guru-disciple relationship, then we have also found ourselves to be the recipients of India's greatest gift, and indeed to have found the very heart of her spiritual offering.

What threads weave together the lives of all the interviewees, other than their having found such a guru, is their long-term adherence to the practices given by that One. Their commitment to *sadhana* uniquely distinguished them from those who had an appreciation for a simple life of wandering, centered on few responsibilities, and ganja smoking in an exotic environment. Many of those I met in the latter category had the external appearance of *sadhuism* but lacked any real inspirational quality. I did meet a couple of exceptions from this generalization—one of whom is interviewed here—and certainly a particular use of intoxicants has always had a place in Indian spiritual culture. However, this is for precise and skilled transformational processes that Westerners and many Indians seem less than ready or equipped for. If one is not able to "ride" the intoxicant then it "rides" us, leading to the dangers of physical addiction. This brings the risk of damage to the body's subtle energetic system; the very system needed to hold transformational energies within us. In Varanasi, widely considered the holiest power place in all India, I saw many Westerners effectively cut off from the real and potent spirit of the place by the inevitable mental and emotional fog created by ganja, opiates, and other psychotropic substances.

On the issue of renunciation, all the interviewees were clear that it is attachment to, rather than possession of, externals that is inhibiting to the process of unfoldment. Surely this includes a dogmatic approach to one's chosen path, fanaticism and fundamentalism being ever-present dangers as long as ego is the predominant force within us. In the preparation of this book I met one or two people who expressed this kind of closed-minded zealousness, and I chose to omit these interviews as being contrary to the real spirit of India's wisdom traditions.

Still, the witnessing of such strongly opinionated individuals serves to highlight where we also may hold such attitudes, and demonstrates the uselessness of them. Value can be extracted from all situations, but, in this instance, I spare readers this exercise in utilizing their own discrimination!

Sadhus and sannyasins, and the traditions they represent, present variations on the relationship between the position of the individual to the Divine. There are dualistic and non-dualistic approaches, with many, many philosophical and theological standpoints—complex and even seemingly contradictory.

Historically, much blood has been shed over these differences, and a fierce ideological clash continues in some quarters, even today. Too much emphasis on the differences of the *sampradayas* and their respective doctrines is counter-productive—potentially ignoring the valuable realizations each system contains. Such realizations serve to both widen and deepen our appreciation and understanding of our own path and those of others. Within the vastness of India's spiritual milieu there are gurus and lineages that fit neither category exclusively, who weave a cloth of beauty, flexibility, and tensile strength; from acknowledgement and integration of the dualistic as well as the non-dualistic stance. The popular Indian saying, "Which is sweeter, to taste honey or to become honey?" is, after all, an unanswerable question.

# Glossary

**A**

*Acharya.* Religious teacher.

*Advaita.* Non-dualism or monism. The doctrine that declares that there is but One Reality; that the individual self and the Absolute are one.

*Aghori.* Practitioner of left-handed *tantra.*

*Ajna Chakra.* The *chakra* located in the "command center" between the eyes.

*Ananda.* Bliss; Divine intoxication.

*Arati.* The waving of lights before a deity or shrine as an act of worship.

*Ashram.* An open center where spiritual seekers congregate or live around the presence of a Master.

*Atman.* The soul, individual self, and universal self.

*Avatar.* Incarnation of God.


**B**

Baba. Affectionate term for father, often referring to the guru.

Benares. Also known as Kashi or Varanasi. Holy pilgrimage city on the banks of the Ganges where Siva is said to eternally reside.

*Bhagavad Gita.* Principal Hindu scripture.

Bhagavan. God. Also used as an epithet of the guru.

*Bhajan.* Religious music usually accompanied with singing or chanting.

*Bhakta.* A practitioner of the path of divine love.

*Bhakti.* Love of God.

*Bhang lassi.* A sweetened and intoxicating beverage of yogurt and cannabis.

*Bhava.* (*Bhav.*) Feeling; emotional state or mood.

Bodh Gaya. The place where Buddha attained illumination.

Brahma. Creator God.

*Brahmachari*. Religious celibate.

*Bramacharya*. The state of religious celibacy.

Brahman. The Absolute, Supreme Reality.

*Brahmin*. Member of the caste responsible for preservation of the *Vedas*,
 teaching and ritual.


# C

*Chakra*. "Wheel." Subtle energy centers located traditionally at six points in
 the subtle body.

*Chela*. Student of a spiritual master or teacher.


# D

*Darshan*. The sighting of the spiritual master or temple deity.

*Dharma*. Means to attain the ultimate good through performance of one's
 duty. Righteousness, that which supports.

*Dhuni*. Sacred fire tended by a *sadhu*.

*Diksa*. Initiation into a spiritual lineage.


# E

*Ektara*. One-stringed musical instrument.


# G

*Gerrua*. Ochre cloth of a *sannyasin*.

*Ghat*. Steps leading to a river or the coast. A landing place.

Gopala. Baby Krishna.

*Guru*. Spiritual master; any person worthy of veneration.

*Guru seva*. Service to the guru.


# J

*Japa*. Repetition of God's names or a *mantra*.

*Jiva*. An individuated soul.

*Jnana*. Knowledge of God, process of reasoning by which one becomes aware
 of one's inseparability with the Supreme.


198

## K

Kali. Goddess of Destruction and Liberation.

Kali *Yuga.* see *Yuga.*

*Karma.* Action; law of cause and effect.

*Kedgeree.* A cooked-in-one-pot dish of rice, lentils and vegetables.

*Keyala.* Whim or will of the divinely-influenced person.

*Kirtan.* Devotional singing.

Krishna. Incarnation of God who resided in Vrindivan as a cowherd, and
later in Dwaraka as a king. The guru of Arjuna in the *Bhagavad Gita.*

*Kum-kum.* Vermilion colored powder.

Kumbha Mela. Assemblage of *sadhus* and others at Allahbad, Haridwar,
Nasik or Ujain at an auspicious time when the sacred water of the
holy rivers of India come together.

*Kutir.* A hit or small building reserved for *sadhana.*

## L

*Lila.* Divine play of God or the guru; a mystery.

## M

*Mahant.* Head or leader.

Maharaj. Respectful form of addressing the guru; great king.

*Mahatma.* Great soul. A high-souled person.

*Mahavakya.* Great formulae found in the Upanishads concisely stating the
nature of Reality.

*Mandir.* Temple.

*Mantra.* Incantation: word or series or words imbibed with and
corresponding to the energy of the Supreme.

*Math.* Monastery.

*Maya.* Cosmic illusion on the account of which ignorance of the soul's
identity pervades.

*Mudra.* Symbolic hand-gesture.

*Murti.* An image of a divine form or idol.

*Mutt.* see, *Math.*

## P

*Parikrama*. Circular pilgrim path.

*Prarabdha Karma*. Residue karma from previous births or actions that have begun to bear fruit.

*Prasad*. Food or other item blessed by the guru or temple deity.

*Puja*. Ritualistic worship.

*Pujari*. Priest.

*Purana*. Holy ancient text covering ritual, myth, cosmology.

## R

Radha. Intimate companion of Krishna.

Rama. Incarnation of God. Hero of the *Ramayana* considered to be the ideal king, husband, and friend.

*Ram Lila*. Play of God.

*Rani*. Queen. Honorific female title.

*Rasa*. Essence; taste; aesthetic mood.

*Ras Lila*. A sacred dance in which Krishna duplicates himself to partner all the *gopis*.

*Rishi*. A seer of truth. Those to whom the *Vedas* were revealed.

## S

*Sadguru*. True spiritual master.

*Sadhaka*. Spiritual aspirant.

*Sadhana*. Spiritual practice or discipline.

*Salagram*. A stone emblem or deity.

*Samadhi*. Absorption into the Infinite. Place where a saint is entombed.

*Sampradaya*. Ascetic sect.

*Samsara*. The world. The cyclic existence of birth and death.

*Samskara*. Mental impressions or tendencies formed from previous actions and experience.

*Sannyasa*. Renunciation of the world and attachments.

*Sannyasin*. One who has renounced worldly life and values.

*Satsang*. Company of the wise.

*Shakti*. Divine energy.

Shankaracharya. Revered sage who expounded Advaita Vedanta the doctrine of non-duality. Great reformer of the Vedic religion.

*Shree yantra.* A cosmic diagram used for meditation, emblematic of the
    Goddess.

Siva. God of destruction and liberation.

*Smarta.* Followers of the traditions established by Shankaracharya.

*Swami.* Lord. Respectful title given to renunciates.


# T

*Tantra.* A system of transformational spiritual practices.

*Tapas.* Austerity; ascetic endeavor.

*Tilak.* A decorative marking placed in the middle of the brow in the position
    of the *ajna chakra.*

*Tucket.* Wooden day bed.


# U

*Upanishad.* Last portion of the *Vedas.*


# V

*Vaishnava.* Generally dualistic worshippers of Vishnu.

*Vedas.* Sacred and authoritative Hindu scriptures.

*Vedanta.* One of the six systems of Hindu philosophy; it literally means "the
    end of the Vedas."

Vrindivan. The town and pilgrimage center where Krishna is said to have
    played as a child and youth.


# Y

*Yoga.* Union of the individual soul and the universal soul. Method of practice
    to that aim.

*Yuga.* A cycle or world period. There are four ages or *yugas* according to
    Hindu philosophy: Satya, Treta, Dwapara, Kali. The first *yuga* is known
    as a golden age of peace and wisdom, successively diminishing in
    virtue until our present age, the Kali *yuga*—commonly known as
    the age of chaos and destruction. The *yugas* are cyclic.

# OTHER BOOKS BY HOHM PRESS

**THE YOGA TRADITION:**
*Its History, Literature, Philosophy and Practice*
by Georg Feuerstein, Ph.D.
Foreword by Ken Wilber

A complete overview of the great Yogic traditions of Raja-Yoga, Hatha-Yoga, Jnana-Yoga, Bhakti-Yoga, Karma-Yoga, Tantra-Yoga, Kundalini-Yoga, Mantra-Yoga and many other lesser known forms. Includes translations of over twenty famous Yoga treatises, like the *Yoga-Sutra of Patanjali*, and a first-time translation of the *Goraksha Paddhati*, an ancient Hatha Yoga text. Covers all aspects of Hindu, Buddhist, Jaina and Sikh Yoga. A necessary resource for all students and scholars of Yoga.

"Without a doubt the finest overall explanation of Yoga. Destined to become a classic." – Ken Wilber

Paper, 708 pages, over 200 illustrations, $39.95
ISBN: 0-934252-83-1
Cloth, $49.95   ISBN: 0-934252-88-2

**FACETS OF THE DIAMOND: THE WISDOM OF INDIA**
by James Capellini

Anyone who has ever felt the pull of India's spiritual heritage will find a treasure in this book. Contains rare photographs, brief biographic sketches and evocative quotes from contemporary spiritual teachers representing India's varied spiritual paths—from pure Advaita Vedanta (non-dualism) to the Hindu Vaisnava (Bhakti) devotional tradition. Highlights such well-known sages as Ramana Maharshi, Nityananda, and Shirdi Sai Baba, as well as many renowned saints who are previously unknown in the West.
Text in three languages—English, French and German

Cloth, 224 pages, $39.95, 42 b&w photographs
ISBN: 0-934252-53-X

## THE ALCHEMY OF TRANSFORMATION
by Lee Lozowick

Foreword by: Claudio Naranjo, M.D.
A concise and straightforward overview of the principles of spiritual life as developed and taught by Lee Lozowick for the past twenty years in the West. Subjects of use to seekers and serious students of any spiritual tradition include: • From self-centeredness to God-centeredness • The role of a Teacher and a practice in spiritual life • The job of the community in "self"-liberation • Longing and devotion. Lee Lozowick's spiritual tradition is that of the western Baul, related in teaching and spirit to the Bauls of Bengal, India. *The Alchemy of Transformation* presents his radical, elegant and irreverent approach to human alchemical transformation.

Paper, 192 pages, $14.95     ISBN: 0-934252-62-9

## THE MIRROR OF THE SKY
*Songs of the Bauls of Bengal*

Translated by Deben Bhattacharya
Baul music today is prized by world musicologists, and Baul lyrics are treasured by readers of ecstatic and mystical poetry. Baul music, lyrics, and accompanying dance reflect the passion, the devotion and the iconoclastic freedom of this remarkable sect of musicians and lovers of the Divine, affectionately known as "God's troubadours."

*The Mirror of the Sky* is a translation of 204 songs, including an extensive introduction to the history and faith of the Bauls, and the composition of their music. It includes a CD of authentic Baul artists, recorded as much as forty years ago by Bhattacharya, a specialist in world music. The current CD is a rare presentation of this infrequently documented genre.

Paper, 288 pages, $24.95 (includes CD) ISBN: 0-934252-89-0
CD sold separately, $14.95

## FOR LOVE OF THE DARK ONE: SONGS OF MIRABAI
Revised edition
Translations and Introduction by Andrew Schelling

Mirabai is probably the best known poet in India today, even though she lived 400 years ago (1498-1593). Her poems are ecstatic declarations of surrender to and praise of Krishna, whom she lovingly calls "The Dark One." Mira's poetry is as alive today as it was in the sixteenth century—a poetry of freedom, of breaking with traditional stereotypes, of trusting completely in the benediction of God. It is also some of the most exalted mystical poetry in all of world literature, expressing her complete surrender to the Divine, her longing, and her madness in love. This revised edition contains the original 80 poems, a completely revised introduction, updated glossary, bibliography and discography, and additional Sanskrit notations.

Paper, 128 pages, $12.00                    ISBN: 0-934252-84-X


## GRACE AND MERCY IN HER WILD HAIR
*Selected Poems to the Mother Goddess*
by Ramprasad Sen; Translated by Leonard Nathan and Clinton Seely

Ramprasad Sen, a great devotee of the Mother Goddess, composed these passionate poems in 18th-century Bengal, India. His lyrics are songs of praise or sorrowful laments addressed to the great goddesses Kali and Tara, guardians of the cycles of birth and death.

Paper, 120 pages, $12.00                    ISBN 0-934252-94-7

**AS IT IS**
*A Year on the Road with a Tantric Teacher*
by M. Young

A first-hand account of a one-year journey around the world in
the company of a tantric teacher. This book catalogues the trials
and wonders of day-to-day interactions between a teacher and
his students, and presents a broad range of his teachings given
in seminars from San Francisco, California to Rishikesh, India.
*As It Is* considers the core principles of tantra, including non-duality,
compassion (the Bodhisattva ideal), service to others, and transformation within daily life. Written as a narrative, this captivating book
will appeal to practitioners of any spiritual path. Readers interested
in a life of clarity, genuine creativity, wisdom and harmony will
find this an invaluable resource.

paper, 725 pages, 24 b&w photos, $29.95     ISBN: 0-934252-99-8

**MARROW OF FLAME**
*Poems of the Spiritual Journey*
by Dorothy Walters
Introduction by Andrew Harvey

Dorothy Walters' compilation of 105 new poems is a rare documen-
tation of a nineteen-year interior journey initiated by her spiritual
awakening.

"What Dorothy has accomplished in this subtle and ravishing
masterpiece is something that many modern poets have been strug-
gling for but without success—a book of poems that work both as a
canny literary artifact and mystical utterance and inspiration."
    —Andrew Harvey

Paper, 156 pages, $12.00
ISBN: 0-934252-96-3

## HALFWAY UP THE MOUNTAIN
The Error of Premature Claims to Enlightenment
by Mariana Caplan
Foreword by Fleet Maull

Dozens of first-hand interviews with students, respected spiritual
teachers and masters, together with broad research are synthesized
here to assist readers in avoiding the pitfalls of the spiritual path.
Topics include: mistaking mystical experience for enlightenment;
ego inflation, power and corruption among spiritual leaders; the
question of the need for a teacher; disillusionment on the path . . .
and much more.

"Caplan's illuminating book . . . urges seekers to pay the price of
traveling the hard road to true enlightenment." —Publisher's Weekly

Paper, 600 pages   $21.95                 ISBN: 0-934252-91-2


## THE WOMAN AWAKE
*Feminine Wisdom for Spiritual Life*
by Regina Sara Ryan

Through the stories and insights of great women of spirit whom
the author has met or been guided by in her own journey, this book
highlights many faces of the Divine Feminine: the silence, the
solitude, the service, the power, the compassion, the art, the darkness, the sexuality. Read about: the Sufi poetess Rabia (8th century)
and contemporary Sufi master Irina Tweedie; Hildegard of Bingen,
Mechtild of Magdeburg, and Hadewijch of Brabant: the Beguines
of medieval Europe; author Kathryn Hulme *(The Nun's Story)* who
worked with Gurdjieff; German healer and mystic Dina Rees . . .
and many others.

Paper, 35 b&w photos; 520 pages, $19.95
ISBN: 0-934252-79-3

## THE ALCHEMY OF LOVE AND SEX
by Lee Lozowick
Foreword by Georg Feuerstein, Ph.D.

Lozowick recognizes the immense confusion surrounding love and
sex and tantric spiritual practice. Preaching neither asceticism nor
hedonism, he presents a middle path grounded in the appreciation
of simple human relatedness. Topics include: • what men want from
women in sex, and what women want from men • the development
of a passionate love affair with life • how to balance the essential
masculine and essential feminine • the dangers and possibilities of
sexual Tantra. . .and much more. The author is an American "Crazy
Wisdom teacher" in the tradition of those whose enigmatic lives and
teaching styles have affronted the polite society of their day.
Lozowick is the author of 14 books in English and several in French
and German translations only. " . . . attacks Western sexuality with
a vengeance." —*Library Journal.*

Paper, 312 pages, $16.95
ISBN: 0-934252-58-0


## THE SHADOW ON THE PATH
*Clearing the Psychological Blocks to Spiritual Development*
by VJ Fedorschak
Foreword by Claudio Naranjo, M.D.

Tracing the development of the human psychological shadow from
Freud to the present, this readable analysis presents five contemporary approaches to spiritual psychotherapy for those who find
themselves needing help on the spiritual path. Offers insight into the
phenomenon of denial and projection.

Topics include: the shadow in the work of notable therapists; the
principles of inner spiritual development in the major world religions; examples of the disowned shadow in contemporary religious
movements; and case studies of clients in spiritual groups who have
worked with their shadow issues.

Paper, 300 pages, 6 x 9; $17.95
ISBN: 0-934252-81-5

# RETAIL ORDER FORM FOR HOHM PRESS BOOKS

NAME_____

ADDRESS_____

CITY _____ STATE _____

ZIP_____

| QTY | TITLE | ITEM PRICE | TOTAL PRICE |
|-----|-------|------------|-------------|
| | **BOOKS** | | |
| _____ | THE YOGA TRADITION - paperback | $39.95 | _____ |
| _____ | THE YOGA TRADITION - hardcover | $49.95 | _____ |
| _____ | FACETS OF THE DIAMOND | $39.95 | _____ |
| _____ | ALCHEMY OF TRANSFORMATION | $14.95 | _____ |
| _____ | MIRROR OF THE SKY - WITH CD | $24.95 | _____ |
| _____ | MIRROR OF THE SKY - CD only | $14.95 | _____ |
| _____ | FOR LOVE OF THE DARK ONE | $12.00 | _____ |
| _____ | GRACE AND MERCY | $12.00 | _____ |
| _____ | HALFWAY UP THE MOUNTAIN | $21.95 | _____ |
| _____ | THE WOMAN AWAKE | $19.95 | _____ |
| _____ | THE ALCHEMY OF LOVE AND SEX | $16.95 | _____ |
| _____ | MARROW OF FLAME | $12.00 | _____ |
| _____ | THE SHADOW ON THE PATH | $17.95 | _____ |
| _____ | AS IT IS - paperback | $29.95 | _____ |

**SURFACE SHIPPING CHARGES**
1st book ............................ $5.00
Each additional item .......... $1.00

**SHIP MY ORDER**
- ☐ Surface U.S. Mail—Priority ☐ UPS (Mail + $3.00)
- ☐ 2nd-Day Air (Mail + $5.00) ☐ Next-Day Air (Mail + $15.00)

**METHOD OF PAYMENT:**
- ☐ Check or M.O. Payable to Hohm Press, P.O. Box 2501, Prescott, AZ 86302
- ☐ Call 1-800-381-2700 to place your credit card order
- ☐ Or call 1-520-717-1779 to fax your credit card order
- ☐ Information for Visa/MasterCard order only:

Card #_____–_____–_____–_____

Expiration Date

| | |
|---|---|
| SUBTOTAL | |
| SHIPPING | |
| TOTAL | |

**Visit our Website to view our complete catalog: www.hohmpress.com**

**ORDER NOW! Call 1-800-381-2700 or fax your order to 1-520-717-1779.**